# THE VIGILANT
# PRINCIPLE

Mark Karsten

 FriesenPress

Suite 300 - 990 Fort St
Victoria, BC, V8V 3K2
Canada

www.friesenpress.com

**Copyright © 2018 by Mark Karsten**
First Edition — 2018

ISBN
978-1-5255-0341-2 (Hardcover)
978-1-5255-0342-9 (Paperback)
978-1-5255-0343-6 (eBook)

*1. FICTION, ACTION & ADVENTURE*

Distributed to the trade by The Ingram Book Company

That old, familiar feeling in the gut, rolling around and poking its way through your insides. You probably know the one: when you're looking for something, and it ends up being right under your nose.

I've spent twelve years searching for a purpose, one that has refused to present itself. I've worked lowly janitorial jobs at middle schools, cleaning up after hundreds of little brats. I've moved up the ranks in a small business, even went so far as to consider opening my own fishing store. That is, until I realized I hated fishing.

Even more than that, I hate the human interaction that comes with owning a store. I could fake it enough to manage one, but the responsibility of ownership seemed daunting.

The number of pipe dreams I've picked up and dropped within the same year would bring shame to my parents, if they weren't long gone. For the life of me, I could never find anything to pour my heart into. I started convincing myself that I simply lacked the conviction, which seemed to come so easy to everyone else.

The realization that you've spent years working but have gotten nowhere is enough to tear a man apart. In my case, there were times that it definitely did. Pieces of me lie along the road I've walked so far, and I never worked up the courage to turn around and pick them back up. I guess it's too late for that now.

I see people with families walking down the street with their children and think that I probably should have worked harder for something resembling normalcy. Seeking a significant other to dedicate myself to, well, at this point that just seems absurd. My receding hairline and indifference towards the majority of humanity isn't helpful either.

Shit, this is turning into a sob story, and that's not where I intended to go. My life really isn't that bad. I'm alone, sure, but I've learned to enjoy it. I work my day-to-day job roasting and bagging coffee beans for an independent roaster. It's monotonous work, and I know it's not a forever kind of deal, but it keeps me fed and happy enough for now. The owner has taken a liking to me, largely because I show up early, work quickly, and don't call in sick. She's a bit of a nut, and more often than not, there's gin on her breath, but I have no real complaints about her. She leaves me alone.

But of course, as humans are conditioned to do, I'm always looking for something more. Something that makes me feel fulfilled at the end of the day. Something that feels like an accomplishment.

When I'm not working, I'm running. When I'm not working or running, I'm reading. And when I'm not working, running, or reading, I sit in my backyard and stare at the sky, wondering what in the hell I am doing.

I pick up my groceries on Tuesdays. Everybody thinks Sunday is the best day to shop; they think everyone is at home with their families, recuperating for the impending return of the nine-to-five, Monday-to-Friday workweek. Sunday is busy because everybody thinks it's not going to be busy. Tuesday is the prime time to get your groceries. Everybody is pissed off that they are back to work, with the weekend only a glimmering memory. They don't want to go anywhere after work, other than maybe a bar or a restaurant to suffocate their sadness with booze or fried food. Monday would be good for these reasons as well, except on Mondays, people still have the ambition that they are going to drop their bitter attitude and get things done. They do their shopping and they pretend to be chipper about it, but you can tell they have a white-hot ball of depression just waiting to burst forth at any minute, and sometimes it does. The day I saw a woman bent over her cart, weeping while attempting to control her three, beastly little offspring was the day I decided Monday was not going to be grocery day anymore.

It's Tuesday, and I'm in line behind a monster of a woman. I'm not **3** referring to her size. In fact, she's quite tiny. But her actions resemble what I could only imagine those of an overworked and underpaid seventy-year-old receptionist to be. Everything is done with a firm jerk of her hand, and every word released with a disgruntled huff. She places every item on the conveyor as if its sole purpose is to ruin her day. A pack of juice boxes, which I hope are not intended for some poor children she has held captive in her house, threatens to explode and shower the aisle in Hawaiian punch when her tiny hands slam it down. Even through all this, Jill smiles and greets the woman as if they were best friends.

Jill works on till five. She is presumably around my age, somewhere in her mid-thirties, judging by the wrinkles beginning to peek through the skin around her eyes, but she's much prettier than I am. Unlike me, her hairline is not receding. In fact, she has beautiful brown hair that falls in loose curls around her pleasantly chubby cheeks. Whenever I see her, she's wearing a smart blue button up shirt and black jeans. Every Tuesday, I go through till five. Initially, it was because five is my favorite number (it sits in the middle and doesn't bother anybody), but eventually I grew comfortable with Jill and her understanding of the fact that I don't do small talk. For me, she comes the closest to what one would call a friend.

The woman's food is neatly bagged, and she's tapping her foot impatiently while rifling through her wallet.

"That comes to one-hundred-sixty-seven dollars and twelve cents," Jill informs her. "Will you be paying with cash or debit today?"

The woman drops a MasterCard in front of Jill and mumbles something inaudible.

"I'm sorry, ma'am, we don't accept credit cards," Jill says, fear and hesitation beginning to show in her voice.

"What kind of store is this? Twenty-first goddamn century and you don't take credit cards?" Rage spit jumps from the woman's mouth. It showers Jill's face, but she maintains her smile.

"I'm very sorry for the inconvenience. If you'd like to fill out a complaint card, I'll be sure to give it to my manager as soon as I can."

I admire Jill more than just about anybody else I interact with. It's a short list, but I still think that's saying something.

"Debit, then, and don't you dare assume that I would waste my time with a complaint card. I'll be back. I'll speak to your boss in person, and your job will be on the line, you snot-nosed little know-it-all."

Jill punches a few keys on her till without skipping a beat and informs the woman she can swipe or insert her card when she pleases. The woman grumbles something, completes her transaction, rips the receipt from Jill's hand, and leaves.

Jill sighs and takes a deep breath before looking up at me, flashing a welcoming smile, and beginning to ring through my groceries. I try to show my support through my eyes when I smile back, but I can't be sure how well it works. As she swipes eggs and vegetables over the scanner, I get the absurd idea in my head that I should actually say something, maybe something cruel, regarding the woman that just harassed her. Something to brighten her day. But that would go against our entire unspoken agreement: no small talk.

My groceries are bagged and she tells me the total—eighty dollars and twenty cents, as it has been for the last four years—but while I'm passing her the exact amount, as I always do, I'm checking to be sure nobody else is behind me in line, and my mouth opens without any certainty of what it's about to do.

"That woman, she was some kind of awful. Terrible, wasn't she?"

Jill laughs. "Yeah, not exactly a sweetheart. But not everybody can be, I suppose."

Honestly, how is it humanly possible to brush things off like that? I'm genuinely angry about how Jill was just treated, but she seems to have forgotten it already.

"I suppose you're right. Thanks, Jill."

She gives me my receipt and a brighter smile than usual before I   **5**
walk out with my bags in hand.

But my mind still lingers on that horrible little lady.

I've thought about this a lot lately, and I've concluded that everybody has a bit of a vigilante buried inside them. Some manage to bury it deep, a rare few leave a finger or a toe peeking out from the dirt, and even more rare are those that dig it up and command it to walk around.

My persona has been that of a composed man who keeps to himself, gets the work done, and leaves quietly without demanding recognition. Or at least, that's how I see myself. From an outside perspective, I could very well just be that quiet loner who wants nothing more than to be left alone. I can't argue that there isn't some truth in that.

But above the quiet and the reserved, I like to think of myself as decent towards others. I like to pride myself on the fact that I'm not unkind without reason, and that if someone smiles at me, I will smile back. I will act with as much courtesy as can be mustered. I've had hopes that these traits would stand out, that people would leave my company with a smile and think, "Oh, what a pleasant guy," and as self-centred as this may be, I have found myself wishing that certain others had had these same hopes to persuade them towards decency.

More often than not, however, I've found certain people to be indecent seemingly for the sake of it. These are the people that I consider a splinter under the fingernail of the world.

I've lived in the same small town for the entirety of my adult life. Prair Pass lies in that special little place where the mountains meet the prairies. It's the best of both worlds, in my eyes, making me lucky enough to see the prairie sunrise in the east and set nestled behind the pine-covered mountains in the west. When I stand on my front steps and look to the south over the tops of all the houses,

I bare witness to the most beautiful union of landscapes. The dry yellow grass and the lush green trees merge slowly, but if I squint to look far enough, it could appear like they were pieced together like different colored bits of Lego. One would be just as likely to run in to a farmer as a mountaineer in the Pass, though honestly there aren't plenty of either; more shop workers and restaurant employees. Most were attracted, just as I was, to the simplicity and comfort of a small town to call home. Although, I'd heard a handful of teenagers call it Pray Yer Passin' By, and couldn't entirely blame them. But the nickname is rather uninventive, if I'm being honest. It isn't the most progressive or updated place to live, the only new establishment we've seen in a few years is a sushi restaurant near the town centre that is actually doing pretty well for itself. But I enjoy it this way.

My house is humble. It is exactly what I need it to be and nothing more. I've grown quite comfortable in this space, and comfort is a rare and precious thing to me. The black and grey stonework covering the outside makes it feel like a fortress, though the old wooden front door, chipped in a few places on the top and bottom, says otherwise. But when I walk through that door, I always get that sense of home that some people crave their entire lives. To the left of the entry way is my living room, simple and tidy—a coffee table, a couch, a tall lamp in the corner, a couple of bookshelves, and a television. Straight ahead, a glimpse in to the kitchen: the stove and refrigerator lining the back wall of the house, the sink and counter opposite of them against the wall between the living room. To the left of the kitchen is a small room where my washing machine and dryer live, along with bottles of cleaner, brooms, mops, and other miscellaneous things like scissors and tape. The hall to the right leads straight to my bathroom, a glowing white porcelain room with a toilet, small sink, and deep tub with a large square showerhead. The only other door, in the middle of the hallway leading to the bathroom, goes to my room. It's more barren than most, I can only assume, containing only a bed on a frame and a single nightstand. My closet door has a mirror, and my closet contains all my clothes.

My floors are always clean, because I sweep and mop every Thursday after dinner. My fridge is constantly stocked with the same food for my weekly meal plan. My television is rarely turned on, but always clear of dust and fingerprints. The books on my shelf are battered and beaten and yellowed and frayed, but well organized, and I would call them my prized possessions. My coffee table has never—and will never—have a cup ring or water stain, as I am adamant about the use of coasters. This is made much simpler by the fact that I don't often have guests over—ever, really. My house is a one bedroom for a reason. It's comfortable, it's quiet, and it's my own.

I place my bags of groceries on my kitchen counter before sorting them in to my barren refrigerator in their respective places—eggs to the right on the top shelf, almond milk in the door, cucumbers in the crisper. I haven't had dinner yet, and so because today is Tuesday, I leave out the ground turkey, jar of pasta sauce, brown bag of mushrooms, and package of spaghetti to be cooked when I am done putting everything else away. I like Tuesdays. All the ingredients are fresh, and spaghetti is my favorite of the weekly meals, next to Wednesdays. Tomorrow, the leftover spaghetti will be poured into a Pyrex dish, topped with the panko breadcrumbs that I am now transferring from a plastic bag to their own jar, and baked. It re-creates the meal into something even more delicious.

As I'm going through all the motions that have become so regular to me that they barely require thought any more, my mind is on the rude lady from the grocery store. My thoughts drift to unkind things, like breaking several of the eggs in my fridge on her car windshield to sit in the sun and rot. But that's just not the kind of person I am.

Yet, as my pasta water comes to a boil and my stomach exclaims its joy for the food about to enter it, I can't help but think it would feel at least a little bit nice to pour it over her head. Obviously, that's going too far, though. That's much worse than she deserves. At times, I can struggle with finding the line and staying on the right side of it. I'm quite talented when it comes to going too far.

The sauce bubbling on the stove smells great, just as it does every Tuesday, and even though I make it exactly the same every week, I give it a taste anyway. To no surprise, it's the same. It's always the same.

Wednesday is, generally speaking, my favorite workday. People seem to struggle with it because it's the middle of the week and they already feel burnt out, but I guess I must be a pretty positive guy, because I love it. Wednesday is halfway to the weekend, although I don't care much for the weekend. I always find myself without much to do. You can only spend so much time reading, and if I ran any more, I'd probably collapse and die.

Wednesday is going as it typically does. It's quiet, and as the beans roast, I find my mind wandering for a short period before something comes to my attention: it seems I'm the only person here.

That's not good.

That means if somebody comes in to make a purchase, which is rare because we mostly fill large orders, I will have to abandon my post in the back and help a customer.

And wouldn't it so happen that at this very moment, in walks a surly-looking, tiny-thing of a woman, demanding service before she's even fully through the door.

God. Damn it.

Of course it's her. The world is a strange place to hurl the beast from the grocery store at me now, when I've only just managed to begin forgetting her. It might just be time to quit this job. Or perhaps I'll humor both her and myself, give her a chance to redeem herself for her actions.

I find my feet carrying me towards her, while my brain prepares words for her.

"What can I do for you today, ma'am?" I ask smoothly.

A glimmer of recognition flashes across her eyes before she buries it and tells me what she needs.

"Two pounds of something strong. I trust your judgment."

*I see you're not planning on any gracious behavior today, so perhaps I'll give you a special roast*, I think as I walk to the back. I pour a pound each of a couple popular blends into the small vacant roaster we keep empty for these occasions when a customer actually comes in.

"I assume you'll want to grind it yourself?" I shout at the woman over the churning sound of the roaster.

"Of course I will. What kind of question is that?" she snaps back.

"Well, you're going to be waiting about ten more minutes," I tell her as I approach the front counter again.

"What, you think I have all day to sit around and wait for you?" she yells.

I'm not going to stand for this much longer.

"Look, it takes as long as it takes. There's nothing I can do," I say.

She huffs and puffs before storming out the door. I'm unsure if that means she wants to cancel her order or she just couldn't stand waiting in the building for a measly ten minutes. Probably a good thing for the both of us, as snapping at her would not be good for my state of employment.

I allow the roast to finish, and it actually smells pretty damn good. While I'm scooping and bagging the beans, I consider objects I could sneak in there to mess with her day. There's a garbage in the back that hasn't been changed in about a week; I'm fairly certain I saw an old brown apple core in there this morning. But that would be too obvious. While I'm trying to decide what to do, she bursts through the front door again.

"Where is my damned coffee? It's been fifteen minutes, and I demand service!" She's shouting like a banshee.

Still, there's nobody else to help her, so that falls on my shoulders. I grab her bag of coffee and approach the front. As she screams words that I don't care to hear, I can feel something inside of me snap.

It's almost as if, throughout my life, I'd put a cap on a lot of the emotions that I simply wouldn't allow myself to feel. Probably a defense mechanism from when I was younger. But at that moment, as my heart rate quickens and the hair on my arms stands up, something hot wells up in my chest. I'd like to call it hatred, but that would oversimplify the thing. It's a pressure that demands to be released, to smash the dam and unleash all that had gathered behind it. I try to breathe, to process my anger by not processing it at all, and shove it down with the rest of it all, but there's just no more room for anything else. This moment, of all the moments in my life, has somehow become my so-called breaking point.

As I approach the woman, I feel calmer than I remember being for a long time. Hell, I'm *grinning* at this horrible bitch. I think it might be a bit scary for her, only she can't fully realize her feelings until I'm standing across the counter, leaning over her and speaking with a threatening calm while staring daggers directly through her eyes and in to the depths of whatever poor excuse for a soul she has in there.

"You need to shut the hell up right this second, ma'am." My face is so close to hers that I can feel warmth coming off her wrinkly old skin.

She gasps, trying to grab words of rebuttal, but she doesn't come up with anything. Instead, she just breathes rancid breath into my face. This is, strangely, the absolute last straw.

"You feel the need to treat others like lesser beings for some reason, don't you? The other day at the grocery store, you were awful to Jill, and she was nothing but pleasant to you."

She finds words, finally. "That's where I recognize you from! I knew I had seen your face before. What gives you the right to speak to an old woman in such a manner?"

"You gave up the right to any decency, from anybody, when you decided to be an inconsiderate old hag. I don't care about your age or your reason; it is unacceptable to act that way." I can't remember the last time I've spoken this much, and as that thought crosses my mind, I decide that will be my final word.

I open her bag of coffee *slowly* and look her in the eyes. I tip the bag directly over her head and allow the still hot coffee beans to spill out. They get stuck in her curled hair and they fall down her blouse, but mostly they simply bounce off and cascade to the floor. She just stares at me in disbelief.

It would seem I've finally managed to shut her up.

I untie my apron calmly, throw it in her face, and walk out of my job. Something has changed in me, and goddamn, do I ever love the way it makes me feel.

I'm in my car on my way home, ecstatic that I just sent my life into a dramatic spiral, though whether it's upwards or downwards has yet to reveal itself. This excitement must be draining, however, because it's only four in the afternoon and I'm hungry as hell. As if by the grace of some God I don't believe in, a burger chain appears on my right; I don't even care which one it is. Their sign is nothing more than a giant, flashing hamburger. I haven't eaten fast food in years, literally years, but I mean, fuck it, I'm already out of control today; I might as well let it continue. I pull into the drive through and order two burgers, big ones, and more fries than a single person should be permitted, with the biggest and bubbliest cola they could give me. I think my total comes to something like twenty-three dollars, but I'm not fazed. For a second, my brain goes to my budget and the fact that I'm stepping outside of it, but I wipe that away quickly with the image of that woman's face as coffee beans bounced off it.

I don't even wait until I get home to eat, which is odd for me, as eating in front of people is usually a huge trigger for anxiety, and the fast food parking lot isn't exactly empty. But I just don't give half a damn right now, and it feels so good that I can't help but go with it.

The first burger is half gone already, two beef patties dripping grease on my pants and strangely colored sauce threatening to drop before I catch it smoothly with my tongue.

I haven't been this pleased with myself in ages, and I don't want it to stop. Really, I don't think it should have to.

There's always going to be bad people in the world. Why not take it upon myself to give some of that indecency back to them? Hell, if it makes me feel this good along the way, isn't that just an added bonus?

Helping people by hurting people never sounded so swell.

I finish my victory meal without an ounce of shame, regardless of the sharp, artery-clogging pain in my chest. I return home and go to sleep, without a care that it's still daytime. I sleep in absolute peace with a calm, quiet mind.

* * *

*Jill*

Late nights aren't exactly a common thing for Jill. She didn't actively try to avoid them, it just never seemed appealing to her, staying up in to the late hours of the night. If a good movie on the TV or an exceptionally attention grabbing chapter of a book managed to pull her in, she might stay up to the wild time of 10:30, but other than that she was often in bed by 9. But tonight, her brain refused to quit.

To be nervous had become something rare for Jill. She'd settled in to a life that she enjoyed, which she found comfortable and simple. She didn't have trouble stepping outside of her creature comforts, but she also didn't feel compelled to do so often.

Seeing someone selflessly stand up for another person had always been one of those things she'd imagined only happening in fiction, let alone happening to her. But she saw no reason why that should make her feel nervous.

She'd interacted with him on so many occasions, though they were always silent, not interrupted with unnecessary niceties or conversations, that she felt a sort of closeness to him. It was easy to exchange not words, but something else, with him, and easy was precisely how Jill had always liked things.

She rolled over in her bed and switched on her lamp. It illuminated her bedside table and the constant stack of paperbacks she kept on hand. Her white walls glowed pleasantly in the dim light, just enough to read under without straining her eyes. She stacked up the only two pillows on her bed, and rested her back against them, picking up one of the three books she'd been reading for the past couple months. Flipping to her page and removing the bookmark, she took a deep breath and let her eyes begin to scan the page, not so much reading as trying to quiet her often calm brain.

\* \* \*

But of course, that calm cannot last. I'm thrown upwards and awake by the sound of my telephone ringing, which is quite an unfamiliar sound and takes my tired brain a moment to recognize. The only people that make any sense to be calling me is work, so I prepare for the conversation, reminding myself that I don't give a damn. I've got a new lifestyle to carry out, and I won't let their guilt trip sway me from my goals.

I get up from bed slowly, pulling on a t-shirt from my pile of unwashed laundry. Although it's laundry day, I don't see it being done today. The phone continues to ring. I don't care much if they are forced to call back a time or two. I feel no need to impress them anymore, and although I do feel bad for causing inconvenience, I know they will be fine without me. Or at least, I suspect they will. If not, I can always go in to help. I snap myself out of that mentality before clicking the green button on the still ringing phone.

"Good morning," I say.

"Morning? It's nearly noon. Where are you? This isn't like you!"

I can almost smell the gin through my telephone. My boss has never raised her voice like this towards me. Is it actually that late in the day? I can't fathom sleeping close to eighteen hours. But somehow, it seems, I've done it.

"Yeah, I know. I'm really sorry. I think I've had a change of heart about my employment with you."

"Hold on a second, what the hell happened yesterday? A woman has been in here since we opened complaining that you yelled at her and then dumped coffee all over her. The beans on the floor don't help your case. What did you do?"

"I dumped coffee all over her. I may have also called her an inconsiderate old bitch. But, if I'm speaking with absolute candor, I don't regret it in the slightest. She *is* an inconsiderate old bitch."

"You can't just say things like tha—"

"Sorry," I say, cutting her off, "but I won't be coming in today. Or any other day, probably. If you desperately need help with anything, call me. If not, I'm afraid to say that this is me quitting. Thank you, and take care."

I hang up the phone. I feel bad for my boss. She's never wronged me, but the progress I need to make will not make everybody happy. I only hope the wrongdoers will feel more of my wrath than the innocent bystanders. But sometimes people will get hurt, regardless of whether I or anybody else wants them to or not.

It's impossible not to notice that my back doesn't hurt and my knees don't creak when I get out of bed and walk to the kitchen. My head isn't throbbing. Most mornings are spent in some mild form of agony before the painkillers take effect and the coffee wakes me up,

but I don't think I need those things this morning. I don't think I'll
need them at all anymore.

The decision of whether or not to stop at dumping coffee beans on
the woman was a difficult one. I labored over it for several days. She
was the one who decided her own fate when she happened to be in
my grocery store on my shopping day.

I decide to do something else different, something I haven't done
in who knows how long. I abandon my grocery list and decide to
buy whatever I want. Funnily enough, my purchases end up being
largely the same as when I stick to the list. My main deviation is
going down the frozen food aisle to find a box of chicken nuggets,
which is where I come upon the woman again.

She doesn't notice me, which I decide is a good thing, something
I should maintain. I keep my distance, quiet as a corpse following her
down the aisles, ducking behind stacked boxes of cereal or cardboard
displays of deodorant when she stops to select something. I do my
best to give her no reason to turn around and look in my direction.

She still wears the same scowling face—no change there. What
I really want to see is how she acts towards sweet Jill. That will be
the true test of whether or not her character has changed since my
outburst. I pursue her through the rest of the store, slowly of course.
This woman's eating habits are disgusting, and it's rather surprising
she hasn't dropped dead yet.

Then I remember the juice boxes, and the idea that she may have
kids, or even grandkids that come to visit. That softens my resolve
to wrought justice all over her stupid head, but only for a moment.
Most people have kids. Most people her age have grandkids. That
doesn't change the fact that they must face the music at some point.

Or maybe the crazy bitch just likes juice boxes.

She's moving through the store so slowly that I begin to grow
hungry, and all the food in the cart only makes it worse. I act impul-
sively, picking out some peculiar looking deli sushi; the package

assures me it was made fresh that day. I break the sticker sealing it shut and pop a piece in my mouth. It's not bad, by any means, but while I'm chewing, I realize that I distracted myself. Though only for a moment, it was long enough for her to make her escape. I scan the deli area, the breads, and the produce, but she is nowhere to be found. I can only assume she has finally finished her shopping.

Now, I know that Jill works till number five, but at times, depending on how busy the store is, a sweet elderly woman may or may not be working till three.

I have to rely on luck to force the woman to till five. I have a feeling she will make that choice, as her attitude seems to be especially poor towards anyone younger than she is, and she seems to enjoy being terrible.

As I cruise my cart slowly past till three to see it empty, I feel a minor foreboding. I find the woman at till five, quietly placing items on the conveyor, while Jill scans them with a smile. I can see fear hiding behind her eyes when she glances at the woman for the shortest second she can manage.

Hopeful old me starts to feel better when I notice she's not slamming things down like she did last week, and she's not huffing nearly as much. Jill smiles at me, as if we're both waiting for the same thing. We won't have to wait all that long, of course. Those that are horrible will remain horrible.

Everything is scanned through, bagged, and waiting to be taken home, but now the same issue that arose last time has come again: payment. Again, Jill asks if she would like to pay with cash or debit and, again, the woman drops a credit card in front of her.

"I'm sorry, ma'am, but as I told you last week, we do not accept credit cards," Jill tells her.

"You haven't gotten your goddamned credit card machines working yet? What are you people, some lazy slobs?"

"Nothing is broken. We just don't accept credit cards. We have never accepted credit cards." Jill's patience is wearing thin, and for the first time I can see anger rising in her cheeks.

"That's not what you told me last week!" The woman is shouting in Jill's face, leaning forward on her toes in an attempt to make up for her small stature. "Your manager—get me your manager now. This is the last straw."

Jill is about to respond, while still maintaining her composure, when I interrupt her.

"That is exactly what she told you last week, actually," I say.

The woman obviously still has not noticed me. She begins to speak while she is turning to face me, but clamps her mouth shut when her eyes meet mine. She looks scared, and I'd be lying if I said I didn't like it a little bit.

"What are you doing here?" she asks after a pause. "Are you following me? I ought to call the police on you, you damned lunatic!"

"You ought to pay for your groceries and leave quietly," I say. I give her a sarcastic smile. I'm going for a menacing look, and I feel I've succeeded when she drops her eyes to the floor and hands over her debit card like a child being threatened with detention.

Jill looks at me with obvious confusion. She knows me as the quiet guy, the one that smiles and nods and gets on his way. This new person that I have become shocks her, as it shocks me. I hadn't prepared to say what I said to the woman; it just poured out. Jill takes the woman's debit card, inserts it into the machine, and hands it over, all the while staring at me and eventually smiling widely.

The woman picks up her grocery bags, shoots me one final glare—which I return with a smile—and is on her way out the door.

"Are you feeling okay?" Jill asks me, laughing.

"Better, really. I feel great," I tell her. "She did deserve it, didn't she?"

For a moment, I question my motives, but only for a moment, because Jill responds.

"She did. I'm glad you said something. I appreciate it. I could only hold it in for so much longer, and I probably would have been fired. So, you saved my job, I guess."

"Thanks for reassuring me."

She begins to scan my groceries, eyeing the things I generally don't buy with curiosity.

"You know, I see you every week, but we've never formally met." She presents her hand across the till. "I'm Jill."

I shake her hand gently, after wiping the sweat from my own, and introduce myself politely.

"It's a pleasure to formally meet you, Jill." I smile at her.

She continues scanning my groceries in silence, glancing up at me every so often, and for the smallest fraction of a second, I consider that she may be as interested in me as I am in her. But, of course she's not. I'm just the methodical man in the grocery store. I may have stood up for her, and that's probably why she's smiling at me, but anyone with any decency would have done the same.

"Straying from the usual lot today, aren't you?" she teases me. "I hope you've still got exact change."

So, she has been paying attention. She probably thinks I'm insane. Perhaps she's even a bit frightened of me, and that's why she always treats me so kindly. I chuckle nervously.

"Yeah, well. I decided it was time to live a little, I guess." I suppose I really have decided that.

Then something else dawns on me: I definitely do not have exact change. I'm just stepping outside of my usual boundaries left and right. I check my wallet to make sure my debit card is there. When I find it, I pretend to throw it at Jill, mocking the old woman. I realize, as I'm doing it, that I'm not funny, and this is a horribly awkward thing for me to do. I stop and stare at my feet until Jill is done bagging my items. I do hear a quiet giggle from her, however, and even though it's likely out of pity, it does make me feel a bit better.

When it comes to payment, I hand over my debit card, only this time I do so like a normal, respectable adult. My hand shakes gently as I pass over my card, and Jill gives me a look I haven't seen on her face before.

"Are you doing okay?" she asks. "You seem a bit, I dunno, different than usual. I don't mean to pry."

I laugh nervously. This is the most personal question I've been asked since I was married, and it's coming from someone that barely knows me.

"Yeah, I'm good, I guess. I've been feeling a bit different lately," I begin, not knowing how much of an answer I should give. "Have you ever just decided to let yourself lose it a bit? Go off track for a while?"

She nods slowly. "Well, yeah. I've thought about it. I can't say I've ever considered seriously acting on it, though. So good for you."

I can't decide if that's genuine or I'm being spoken to like a child, but I don't mind much. I punch in my pin number, my receipt prints, and Jill tucks it into one of the bags. She tells me to have a good day, and it seems as if our conversation is over, so I begin to walk away.

But then I stop.

"Jill, look, I'm not sure exactly who I'm going to be next week. I know that sounds insane, but I'm trying to change my life around. I hope this isn't wildly inappropriate, but I have to say something while I have any inkling of the courage to do so. Do you want to . . ." I pause, realizing that I'm doing exactly what I've wanted to for a long time, and it actually feels okay. "Do you want to do something some time? I don't really know how to do this. Dinner, maybe? Or something like that?"

I take a deep breath to recover from my long-winded request, while she begins to laugh. I assume that's a bad sign, at first, but it turns out to be all right.

"A date, you mean?" she asks.

I hadn't even considered her being in a relationship, for some reason. My ignorance led me to assume she was lonely as I was.

"Yeah, a date. I'm sorry. That was incredibly forward. I don't do this kind of thing." My faux confidence is faltering. I should probably just walk away, find a new grocery store, and never come back.

"I think I would like that," she says.

A concrete block, previously unnoticed, is removed from my shoulders. I look up at her and smile wildly. I feel like a ten-year-old boy, and not even in a cute kind of way—in the foolish and embarrassed sort. I stumble over words before thanking her, and then upon realizing how strange it is to thank someone for accepting an offer of a date, try to take it back, but I achieve nothing more than making things more uncomfortable.

But she laughs about it and everything feels good because she's laughing, so I begin laughing as well.

"Will you pick me up? Should I meet you somewhere? What's the plan?" she asks.

I don't have any answers. I hadn't made any sort of plan.

"Yeah, sure, I don't know. Should I pick you up? We can go to a restaurant. What kind of food do you like?"

There's the foolish little boy again. I'm talking too much now, a problem I have never really had before.

She's still laughing at me, and it still feels good, but she manages to say, "Pick me up from here on Friday evening after six. We can figure out the rest from there."

She smiles and I smile back. Someone has approached her till, so I figure it is an appropriate time to leave. I say goodbye and she waves. I almost forget to pick up my groceries before walking away. I double back, pick up the bags, almost spill the contents of one, wave to her, and get on my way.

I leave the store feeling like I can achieve anything.

I realize when I reach my home that one of the few monotonous habits that I have maintained is grocery shopping on Tuesdays. I have, apparently, intended to ask Jill out on a date for quite some time, without being sure of how or when to do it. I'm very glad that I have.

While I'm putting the groceries away, deciding between chicken nuggets and steak for dinner, it dawns on me that I have no experience in dating and absolutely no idea what to do on Friday. I decide to research some restaurants—put some thought and planning into what we do—so I grab my car keys and walk out the door again. Perhaps I'll test out a couple things from the few different restaurants in town and hope that will help me make a decision.

I make my way downtown, an area I normally don't even think about, to search for a nice-looking place to eat. Prair Pass isn't that large, so the town centre isn't anything to be amazed by, but it's still a bit much for me. I drive by a few restaurants that look nice enough, but nothing really catches my eye. In retrospect, I should have gotten more information from Jill. If she has allergies, we'd have to work around that.

I pull into the parking lot of a sushi place with a big flashing sign off the highway just before the town centre—Tengoku Sushi. There's a line up just outside the front door. It seems safe to assume that it's a pretty popular spot. I contemplate if I'm patient enough to wait, but do I really have anything better to do?

I park and get out of my car, walking slowly up to the line, where a hip looking couple are bobbing back and forth just outside of the tall glass front doors, peering over the heads of the people in front of them. The man shivers, although it's quite a warm night. Just as I'm approaching, the line shifts, and they begin to wiggle their way inside. When I claim their place, leaning in the front door but not quite able to get inside, they notice me and squish together just enough so I can get in and shut the door. I nod at them both, smiling, and voice my thanks. Some like to assume the generation following themselves are all utter assholes, but I'd heartily disagree. There's good and bad in any age. They return the smile and go on with their own conversation.

It only takes fifteen minutes of awkwardly standing alone to get to the front of the line, where I'm informed I can sit at the bar, if that's fine by me, as it is reserved for lone diners. I accept gratefully and am seated in front of a bar with six beer taps to my right and three sushi chefs working quickly and delicately to my left. I have immense admiration for their ability to work under such pressure, and in such a small space. I see one slicing generous pieces of salmon from a larger chunk, and applying it to oval balls of rice with firm yet gentle pressure. He places three of these on a small, square plate, drizzles a squiggle of thick, black sauce in a corner of the plate, and places them in the window behind the bar, quickly tapping a bell to notify the waiter.

I'm handed a menu, and the smallest woman I have ever seen places a glass of water in front of me. She smiles and asks if I'd like anything else to drink. When I say no, she is quickly on her way. Polite and efficient; it's obvious why this restaurant has been doing so well. I peruse the menu quickly, remembering I still have to research a couple other possible restaurants for Friday, and pick out sushi and soup. Almost as soon as my menu is closed, the tiny waitress is back at my side, asking what I would like to eat. I order four pieces of salmon sushi and a half order of their specialty ramen. Although the half order is not on the menu, she makes a note beside the ramen and doesn't question it at all. This will definitely be high on my list of potential date spots.

I wait patiently, sipping my water and watching people, checking out the different menu items placed in front of them. It's impossible for me not to eavesdrop on a loud gentleman and his girlfriend who were seated just after I was. They're still looking through the menu. The man is rubbing his temple, as if he's had a stupendously rough day. The woman smiles and reaches out to hold his hand, but he immediately retracts it and shoots her a 'fuck off' glare. Her smile drops, but only for a moment, as if she's used to this kind of treatment. What a bastard.

"How do you feel about sharing some tempura, sweetie?" she asks him in a cutesy voice.

"Really? You want that deep-fried garbage? What about, like, an edamame salad?"

At this point, my food has arrived, and it proves difficult to force a smile to the tiny waitress after what I've just witnessed. I turn to my food and begin to eat, still keeping my ears open to the table behind me.

"I guess that might be a better idea," the woman says, replacing her sweet voice with a monotone one.

"Of course it would, dear," he says. I can hear him snapping his fingers at their waiter and mumbling a complaint about the poor service, even though their waiter comes over quickly.

He orders for both of them: a salad for his girlfriend and, funnily enough, the tempura and an array of sushi for himself. He even has the audacity to demand his food be brought out within fifteen minutes or he would leave without paying the bill.

I eat slowly and quietly, hoping to pick up on any further conversation they may have, but they don't speak at all. A glance over my shoulder tells me that he is staring at his cellphone and her eyes rest dully on her water glass, the spark in her eyes before has disappeared.

I slurp up the last of my ramen when I hear their waiter dropping off their food. He apologizes politely for the wait, to which the woman responds, "It's totally fine, don't worry. Thank you."

The man says nothing.

I contemplate my last two pieces of sushi. I eat one and continue to listen. They eat without conversation, although the sounds coming from his mouth as he gorges himself are vile. I finish my food, and as my plates are being collected, I ask for a dessert menu.

I don't plan to order from it, but I want to time my departure to coincide with theirs.

She returns with the small square menu, and I look it over slowly, reading every description twice. I'm tempted by the deep-fried green tea ice cream, but I can't risk having to wait for it.

I hear the man belch loudly behind me and snap his fingers again at their waiter. My waitress comes back around, conveniently, at the same time.

"On second thought, can I just have the bill whenever you have a moment?" I ask her. I hate to be an inconvenience, so I put more effort into my smile this time.

She returns with it quickly, and I clear up with cash just as the couple is walking out the door. I walk quickly to catch up with them. Their car seems to be in the opposite direction of mine, and although they couldn't possibly know that, it feels sketchy of me to be following them. The woman glances nervously back a couple of times, clarifying that my feelings must be showing in my mannerisms. The man couldn't be more oblivious. They get to his sleek, black Mercedes, and as he's beginning to open his door, he finally notices me.

"Can I help you with something?" he asks me.

I don't feel this merits a response, so I just continue walking up to him.

I punch him square in the nose before he has a chance to expect anything of the sort. He falls to one knee and starts to sputter something through the blood flowing heavily into his mouth.

"You're an arrogant little fuck," I tell him. My voice is calm. "You can't treat people the way you treat her."

"None of your damn business, old man," he manages to say.

"And you, you can't allow yourself to be treated like that," I tell the woman. She looks ashamed for a second, before nodding at me.

The man is beginning to get to his feet now, so I kick down, strongly, into his kneecap. He lets out a shocked gasp of pain, groaning deeply with every following breath, and doesn't make another attempt to get up. Too arrogant to cry in front of anybody, he buries his face in the crook of his arm and begins to shake and sniffle through short, pained breaths.

"He's right. You can go fuck yourself, Harv," she tells him.

Of course he has a name like Harvey.

We walk away together, leaving him bleeding and cursing in the parking lot. I offer her a ride, but she declines, strongly, and tells me she'll be fine. And I know she will.

Before she walks away, she turns back to me once more. "Look, thank you and all, but don't you think you went a little bit overboard?" Then she leaves.

I feel a wave of shame wash over me. I've never acted out in violence like that. Maybe I did go over the top. Perhaps my actions were unwarranted. Harvey probably won't walk normally again for a long time. I may have just ruined his life.

That really makes me question who the bad guy was in this scenario.

There would have been regret buried in the back of my mind forever if I let him walk away from that restaurant, but I can't say for sure if he deserved what I dealt out. But as soon as I hit him once, I didn't want to stop.

Still, I feel like I want to be booting him in the knee. I have half a mind to turn around and dish out some more, but I don't. I get in my car and drive home.

I've lost any interest in investigating other restaurants. I hope Jill likes Japanese food.

I hadn't anticipated how terrifically boring unemployment would be. The days since I walked out of work have been spent sleeping in, getting up when I want, eating what I want, and doing what I want. Mostly, they crawl by at a painful pace. I've been going to the library, researching what kind of training private investigators need.

Tomorrow is Friday and my nerves are at an incredible high. I've been sweating for the majority of the day. I tried running to divert my attention, but my resting heart rate is already so high I felt as if I was nearing a heart attack just a few blocks from my house.

I tell myself it will be fine, but I've never been that confident, so to deal with it all, I decide to pick up a six-pack. As a compromise, I tell myself I must buy it from the grocery store where Jill is likely working. If I can't manage to stop by on a day that definitely isn't grocery day, just to say hello and pick something up, then how in the world am I supposed to make it through an entire dinner? Seems fair to me.

I rub a stick of deodorant under my armpits but decide against jumping in the shower. I grab my keys from their place by the door and walk to my car.

At every stop sign, I consider turning around, just leaving it be until tomorrow. I consider that it might be creepy of me to just show up the day before our dinner, out of the blue, on an irregular day, but I drive on, wiping my hands on my jeans every couple of blocks. When I come within view of the parking lot, I realize the full extent of my mistake. People are pushing carts every which way, cars are struggling to find spaces, and others are struggling even to pull out of theirs. It's Thursday, and the grocery store is a goddamn warzone.

I park a block away, just to sit and observe for a moment. Even more than before, I just want to go home, but I know if I do, there will be the feeling of failure to deal with. I don't need that right now. My mind is set, and I know I have to do this, if not for the beer then simply to know that I can. My car remains parked where it is; I have no intention of struggling in the lot.

Walking down the rows of parked cars assures me that I've made the right choice. Not a single space is open. The front entrance is a cornucopia of tomfuckery, so I alter my path towards the side entrance where the liquor store lies. When I get to these doors, I see that it's much more within my comfort zone. Barely anyone struggles to get in or out.

There's only one other man inside, old, sad, and obviously an alcoholic, with a large, red, porous nose. The young man working the register says a nonchalant hello without looking up at me.

The small selection of wines attracts my attention for a brief moment before my more cynical side takes over. Perhaps Jill will want to come back to my place for a drink after dinner. Ha. Perhaps not. I wouldn't know what to look for, anyhow, although there are few choices. The beer cooler consists of two large fridges directly beside the entryway that connects this and the grocery store next door. A quick peek shows that people I've never seen before are working the first three tills.

I don't know exactly how to choose a beer, either, which must be quite obvious, because as I uselessly wander past a multitude of brands and labels I don't recognize or have any feelings towards, the young man at the register finally takes notice of me and asks if I could use a hand with anything. I should say yes, but I don't. A number of words that don't mean much to me, in terms of taste, cover the boxes: amber, malt, hops. I pick out a box of six bottles, which aren't overly cheap, but they're nothing too flashy either. There's a moose on the front of a black and gold label. I glance back to the till, as if for reassurance, and I receive a nod of approval. I flash him a quick smile before making my way through to the grocery side.

It's as hellishly busy inside as it was outside. I was hesitant when I peeked through, but I didn't realize the magnitude of what I was diving into. Every till has a line up. Every other person seems to have a child running around and shouting for no apparent reason.

I'm pleased with the changes I'm making in my life, but there is a very good reason I shop on Tuesdays.

With the amount of people buying groceries, I feel as if I should just go back to the liquor store side and make my purchase there, but subconsciously I believe I've been drawn towards even the idea of seeing Jill, if only for a moment. It would make everybody's life so much easier for me to turn around, and it becomes apparent that it would, in fact, be very awkward for me to go through Jill's till at this point. I'm not even positive that she's working. I make a sharp one-eighty and go back from where I came.

"Pretty crazy over there?" The young man at the register says. He seems quite bored, but not at all unhappy about it.

"It's awful," I tell him, while handing over the beer.

He rings them up and I pass over my debit card, still glancing over my shoulder. I hope for even a glimpse of her.

"You come in every Tuesday, don't you?" he asks.

I'm taken aback by the fact that he would notice something like that. He seems more like the float-through-the-day-paying-as-little-attention-as-possible type.

"Yeah, well, I used to, I guess," I tell him. "Kind of stepping outside my comfort zone right now."

"Good for you, man. You gotta step outside the box once in a while, or life gets boring, y'know?"

Am I seriously getting life advice from the twenty-something-year-old kid who works at the liquor store? More than that, though, is it the very advice I've based most of my recent decisions on? Shit. Maybe I've just totally lost it.

"Yeah, you're very right," I say.

When I reach the door, I pause and turn around.

"Hey. Thank you," I tell the young man, smiling, and push the door open directly into Jill's face.

I can't even comprehend what I've done before I'm kneeling down and apologizing over and over again. Her nose is bleeding, but not nearly as badly as the man whose nose I probably broke the other evening. At first, she just groans and squeezes her eyes shut, but then she does something entirely unexpected. She starts to laugh.

"Did you seriously just do that?" She's shaking with giggles now. I can't tell if she's mad, if I've given her brain damage, or if she's genuinely entertained by what just happened.

"I'm so sorry! I didn't see you. I wasn't looking. I just pushed and you were there and then you were on the ground." I go on and on.

"I've forgiven you already, I just can't even believe it; you're the most careful, methodical person I've ever met." She's right about that. Well, my former self, at least.

"I . . . yeah, I don't know what happened. I'm really sorry. Are you okay?" I give her a hand and pull her to her feet.

She pulls her hands away from her nose, which has already stopped bleeding, and laughs again.

"I'm fine, really. Just surprised. What are you doing here, anyways? It's not Tuesday." She notices the beer that I've placed on the ground. "Huh, wouldn't have pegged you for much of a drinker."

I can hear disapproval in her voice. Now I'll be forced to either tell her I'm picking this up in hopes of having a drink in her company tomorrow, or that I'm acting spontaneously and having a beer to calm my nerves. Neither sounds like a good idea right now.

"I'm not, really." I can feel a stutter forcing its way into my words. "I just thought maybe, tomorrow night, if you were interested, that I should be prepared if you wanted to have a drink or something, after dinner."

"Well, if I'm being honest, I don't drink, really. Ever."

I chose the wrong words, obviously.

"But if I were to, I think you'd have better luck with a bottle of wine. A girl's got to feel classy." She laughs, sarcastically, but with a clear effort to calm the nerves that had bubbled up through my words.

I appreciate her effort, but it doesn't help much. My face is getting hot, and sweat is forming on my forehead.

"Yeah, of course. That was stupid of me, sorry."

I wonder if I could return the beer and get wine instead, but remember that the beer initially was for me, although I can't say I want it much anymore. I feel like an absolute fool.

"But let's cross that bridge when we get to it, okay?" she asks.

I nod.

"We're still on for tomorrow, right?"

I nod again. I'm surprised she's still willing to go to dinner with me, considering the fact that I just gave her a bloody nose and acted like a presumptuous douche.

"Of course, if you're still up for it," I say with a smile.

"What, you think you can scare me off with a door to the face and a case of beer?" she asks. "And hey, relax a bit, okay?"

I envy that bold, confident attitude of hers.

"Yeah, you got it," I say. "I'll see you here tomorrow night?"

"Sounds good. Enjoy your beers," she says, winking and walking in the opposite direction.

The young man working at the register glances between Jill and me before letting out a raucous laugh.

"You better step your game up a bit there, dude," he says. His sarcasm makes me regret showing appreciation for his shitty, sage-like advice. But I know he's right. I do have to step up my game.

"Pull your damn act together, old man," I say to myself while I walk to the car.

Old man. I don't know why I just called myself that. Never before have I really considered myself old. That's what that shithead called me the other night before I beat the hell out of him. A pang of guilt threatens me. I don't want to feel that right this second, so I push it down and bury it once again, before driving home. I tell myself he deserved it. He had it coming. I only acted on what others would have thought about—*dreamed* about doing.

I walk through the front door, put all but one of the nearly warm beers into the fridge, and sit down on the couch to collect myself. I twist the top off with a bit of trouble and take a tentative sip. I don't remember my last beer. The carbonation surprises me a bit, and I end up choking and coughing. It's not bad, but I still have to fight to get the first one down. I blame the temperature.

As I drink, I struggle between my heavily inhibited self, and the whimsical vigilante that I'm trying to become. The person I used to be and the person that I'm becoming. The person I am right now is someone torn between the two, I see now. I'm nothing special. It's hard to see which side I'll end up on, but I feel the need to trust myself about what I've been striving for.

With every empty beer bottle that joins the others on my coffee table, I grow more introspective. Lucky for me, in a way, or else the mess on the table would drive me nuts. I consider my past: my experiences, my losses, and how they have come to affect my actions now. Debbie pries her way into my thoughts for the first time in years. Along with her come the tears that I said I wouldn't shed again. Just another promise made to myself that's now broken. Oh well.

The first thing I remember telling myself as an angsty, teenage boy is never to allow myself to be mediocre. I would be okay with becoming nothing, and above all, I wanted to be exceptional, but more than that, I did not want to become just okay.

I realize now that that's exactly what I did. I didn't enjoy much of anything I did, and it showed—nothing I did was special. I had settled in and became something I hated because I was scared. You hear a lot that when you lose someone you love it kills a piece of yourself. Maybe it's the alcohol that's opening my eyes, but it's becoming apparent just how much of me died on the day that she did.

A man, drunk, in the middle of the day, hit Debbie with his car. He shattered her skull, along with most of the rest of her body, and killed her instantly. I wasn't much of a cook back then, but I had made dinner that night. I was going to take a stab at romance, hope to re-ignite some of the fire we had both been too busy for, but she never arrived. What I got instead was a phone call and a debilitating sense of loss. I don't remember much from that period of my life any more. It took time, but I managed to block it out.

All I remember is, for months at a time, staring at the front door, waiting and hoping she would walk through it and tell me it was all a bad joke. She always had a pretty dark sense of humor. I think that's why we worked so well. We could both acknowledge the evil of the world and laugh in its face.

Of course, that's not to say that we didn't want the malevolence to be gone. Only that, if we couldn't get rid of it, we'd do the second best thing: laugh at it.

I'm not half the person I was before she died.

The beer's gone and I'm angry I didn't buy more. With every drink, I grew sadder, but for some reason, I like it, and I want more. I want to take it further, see how down I can get before I fall asleep. The ticking clock is noticeably louder now than ever before. It tells me that it's too late to go back to the store. I've been sitting and drinking much longer than I imagined. I stand up, feeling a minor wobble in my knees, and walk to my bookshelves along the wall to my right. I run my hands across the spines, hoping a title will stick out to me, something to pick up and distract me for the night.

Lately, the books haven't kept my attention, running doesn't distract me, and I've abandoned my jobs. Perhaps I've cut out these things sub-consciously, to untether myself from what's been holding me back.

I want to wipe out the evil women and men that Debbie and I used to despise in our own special way. I'm going to stop laughing, and start kicking.

* * *

Fuck. The headaches. I don't miss these. Those and the unwar-ranted guilt, the turning of my stomach, the dryness on my tongue. Hangovers. They're the worst. I don't miss these feelings, any of them.

I reach to my bedside table where my water glass always is, but of course it's not there. I didn't fill it last night. The circular watermark where the glass always stands affirms how damn monotonous I've been.

I miss it, a bit, although that's probably just the thirst talking.

It's a struggle to remember the last time I had this feeling in my body, and the struggle is made more difficult by the feeling itself. The depres-sion of the night before comes back all at once, and it drags with it embarrassment. I was all by myself, so it doesn't make any sense for me to feel shame, but it's there regardless. It hurts deep in my stomach. A cough forces itself out, and my insides threaten to purge themselves. The remnants of last night's beer sloshes around violently.

I shut my eyes and slowly slide my knees off the bed. As soon as my toes hit the cold floor, aches shoot up through my shins, to my knees, through my hips, and resonate in my back. It hurts to get up. I wince and take a moment before forcing myself to keep walking to the bathroom. Deciding whether I'll puke or just pee is taken out of my hands quickly when I flick on the bright fluorescent bulb. Diving towards the toilet bowl is my first impulse, but I don't. It takes serious concentration and self-control to walk there slowly, crouch down painfully, and let forth a river of bile and foam and some pink substance I don't want to think about.

It hurts, but at the same time, getting it out is strangely blissful. It embodies everything good and evil all at once.

Goddamn, I really must be getting old if a six-pack can put me in this horrible condition. I'm going to have to seriously pull it together if I'm going to make the date with Jill tonight. I stand up slowly and am greeted with a spinning in my head that forces me to lean against the sink. I splash some cold water on my face, which helps, but only for seconds at a time. The cold water running over my hands pulls my attention to a dull throbbing through my knuckles, which are deeply bruised and purple from their introduction to a man named Harvey's face. I get the shower going, not too cold but not too hot, and step in slowly.

I stand under the water, letting it pour over me, feeling the impact of every tiny stream, for what feels like a long time.

I wash away the stink and the shame, and I get out feeling much closer to okay. I brush my teeth thoroughly, floss, and rinse with mouthwash from under the sink. We're getting there.

Strangely, there is a hint of confidence under the haze of this hangover, a feeling that if I can pull it together through this, then things are surely going to fall into place.

## *Jill*

Jill had been having a day that would not stand out in the grand scheme of things. People hadn't been notably horrible, or really anything more than indifferent. She did her job, they did their shopping, and everybody moved on. She likes these kinds of days. They seem to go by quickly. She could function on something close to autopilot and not have to worry about making mistakes. It's been years at the same job. She was simply past the point of caring. Even if she were to make a mistake, the owners would likely overlook it.

She finds it difficult to decide if she's excited for the evening ahead. Either that, or nervous—or downright scared. She just doesn't know how to feel about it. Her last date was years ago, before she started working here. Whether it was the lack of interest in her, or her lack of interest in seeking out a companion, she couldn't know. A combination of the two seems to make the most sense. She was confident enough in her own allure, although anyone who knows her wouldn't guess it.

Jill kept herself in shape. She was on her feet constantly at work. She walked home more often than not, due to her choice not to operate a motor vehicle—she, apparently more than nearly everybody else, realized how much a responsibility it is to hurl several tons of sheet metal and working parts and tires down a road at irresponsible speeds. She didn't drink, or not much, at least. She didn't smoke. She didn't partake in recreational drugs. She never had. She had never wanted to.

Jill did what she wanted, when she wanted. She just didn't often want to do all that much. That's what worked for her. She hadn't always been that way though.

As a child, her parents had constantly pushed her and pressured her to better herself. She was top of her class up until college, which she chose not to attend. Not at first, at least. Although later on, she would go to school and get a bachelor of art in creative writing. She

didn't sell a single page, a single word, and had only recently come close to paying off her student loans.

The grocery store was good for her. It kept the bills paid, kept her busy, and had just enough human interaction to make her not feel like a freak. It also helped her meet him.

In college, she'd dated a guy named Brad. They stuck it out for a year and a half. She genuinely loved him, and he genuinely loved her, but eventually, she started to realize she didn't know who she was without him anymore.

She didn't like that. She'd always known just who she was and just who she wanted to be—losing that was as close to losing everything as she could possibly come. She called it off and told him she needed to maintain her independence. As always, he had understood, but she could see that she had shattered the poor boy's inexperienced heart.

After that, she avoided relationships, avoided hurting someone again. But something about him made her feel okay. She could see in his eyes that he had felt that kind of hurt before, and that, if it came down to it, he would be able to get through it just fine once again. Obviously, she didn't want to hurt anyone, but perhaps a part of her was getting tired of being alone. That cute, incredibly awkward feeling of a first date was something she knew and would admit to missing. Even thinking about it now made her feel funny inside and lifted her lips into a coy smile.

Is that . . . no, it couldn't be. A hint of *excitement*? For a date? Who even am I? Jill shakes her head out of her daydream as a customer approaches her.

"Hello, do you have a club card before I start ringing you through?" Jill asks, getting back into her mindset for work.

\* \* \*

Damn, that was an awfully rough morning. After having something to eat and washing my face in ice-cold water about a hundred times,

I'm finally starting to feel like myself. I'm actually feeling surprisingly optimistic about tonight.

I don't think I'm ever drinking again, however. Not outside of special occasions, at least—which tonight may end up being. I haven't taken part in anything romantic in such a long time that I'm not sure how to act. Jill doesn't seem like the type of person that needs to be pampered. I suppose I'll just have to try to act natural, whatever the hell that means.

\* \* \*

*Ivan*

Detective Ivan Lark considered himself an honest, hard-working man in a department full of lazy, ignorant bastards. He started every day early and ended late. Even, or especially, when there was nothing to do. Ivan would find something, and he would do it exceedingly well. He never received any awards. His wage had remained the same for eight years. Diana, the police chief, rarely even acknowledged his hard work; Ivan presumed it was a tactic to avoid inflation of ego. That's just not the type of person Ivan chose to be. He poured every ounce of himself into his work, because at the end of the day, when he was exhausted and physically incapable of keeping his eyes open, it was much easier to collapse on his couch than it would be to crawl in to a cold lonely bed with a head full of thoughts.

It happened to be one of the days where picking out the real cops from the donut-munching, coffee slurping, beer-gutted men and women was especially simple. An old and pissed off woman stood at the reception desk, tapping her overpainted nails on the desk impatiently. Nobody even seemed to notice her.

He was performing an experiment, testing to see if anyone would realize her presence and go to help her—or at least, how long it would take.

Nobody wants to talk to these types. It was obvious she wasn't in any kind of emotional or physical crisis. It's more likely that she'd been there to complain about some kids riding their bikes across her lawn or pissing in her garden and killing her prized cucumbers. Both serious offences, you can be assured, and of course they'll be looked into, but even Ivan doesn't like giving them immediate attention. He doesn't like to encourage these kinds of people. The only thing that could improve the conversation he's bound to end up having with her is if she feels implored to tell him how to do his job.

There's no doubt that she'll tell him to dust her fence for fingerprints, or make a cast of the bike tire marks on her precious grass. People just don't understand that isn't how things work. This isn't television, and even if it were, they still wouldn't give a damn about her lawn or her vegetables. And even if they truly and deeply DID care, there is no way they would give anybody anything more than a slap on the wrist and a "don't do it again, kid, or there'll be trouble!" to the vile criminal she's reporting.

She's still drumming her nails, clocked in at thirteen minutes without anybody even glancing at her. Persistent old bird, you've got to give her that. Ivan stands from his chair, straightens his back in an effort to ward off the aches, tucks in his shirt, and begins his approach. He flashes the old helpful cop smile at her when eye contact is made, but her scowl doesn't budge. She drums her fingers up until the second he reaches the desk and he begins to speak with as much (still a miniscule amount) charm as he can muster.

"What can I help you with today, ma'am?" he asks.

"I'd like to report an assault. Or harassment. Something like that. Or both, I suppose."

She actually does seem rather shaken up, and Ivan almost begins to regret prior judgments.

"Okay, would you like to come with me and take a seat somewhere more private, and you can tell me all about it?"

"No, I don't want to go anywhere. I'll just tell you here and now."

"Very well. I'll need to get the paperwork for an official report. Would you like a cup of coffee?"

She flinches at the question. "No coffee. Just make it quick, please." She's still frowning. She looks and seems like a real piece of work, but it can't be helped. Ivan feels rather bad for her.

"You got it. I'll be back in just a moment," he tells her, and walks away.

On his specifically planned route, chosen to avoid any contact with the other officers, Ivan feels a slap on his shoulder. He turns and puts on a pissed-off, leave-me-the-hell-alone face. His eyes meet those of Detective Larry Hill, one of the fattest and laziest of the department. Above that, Larry is absurdly unprofessional. His uniform is unbuttoned, leaving his gut—which is threatening to rip through his stained muscle shirt—exposed. A circle of perspiration has formed around his belly button. It makes Ivan feel physically ill.

"Workin' hard as usual, eh, Ivan?"

Ivan isn't the most positive of people, but he notably fucking hates that phrase. He accepts that his coworkers are not going to do any work, but damn them if they try to distract him from doing his.

"As usual, Larry. Excuse me." Ivan gently puts his hand on Larry's shoulder to push him out of the way, and immediately regrets it, as the sweat seeping out of him wets Ivan's palm. He had never witnessed sweaty shoulders before; in fact, he hadn't been sure if it was possible. He winces at the feeling of sticky sweat, and wipes it on his pants in an obvious motion of disgust. He means to—no, he sincerely *hopes* to—offend him.

"We're all going for pints later," Larry says loudly after him, and then more quietly, "you grumpy bastard."

Fuck that guy.

Ivan finishes the last couple of cold mouthfuls in his coffee cup, wishing it was bourbon, and plans on refilling it before going to start this report. But of course, in the break room, there's no coffee. There's no reason to expect there to be; Ivan's coworkers probably don't even know how to make coffee. He drops his cup in the sink and two cracks form on either side of the handle, but he just leaves it there.

He's making his way back when he finally notices just how disheveled the woman looks. Before, it was masked by her aura of pissed-off-old-lady, but now he's heard her voice, and he notices her jump when Larry begins laughing and slaps his hand down firmly on his desk.

Goddamn, Ivan thinks, I've gotten softer and softer every year since I hit forty, but I actually feel a surge of sympathy for her.

He tries to smile supportively when he puts down the report and begins to ask for her information. She answers shortly, as if she wants to be done with this and get back home before Jeopardy, and the sympathy, begins to fade. That is, until she tells him what has happened.

"He just, well, dumped hot roasted coffee beans all over me. It was completely unwarranted. I didn't do anything to deserve it!"

"Are you sure you didn't say anything he could have taken as offensive, ma'am? Nothing condescending or degrading to his profession? Anything like that?"

She doesn't like that question.

"Of course not. Are you dim witted? I'm telling you exactly what happened! Did I say anything at all that would make you think that?"

"Well, you're being rather short with me."

She looks shocked at that, as if Ivan's blown her mind with the simple idea. "But regardless, it would not call for such behavior," he manages to get out before she starts spewing her story once again.

Ivan's mind goes on autopilot for a moment, picking out any important details, but not entirely paying attention. In through the front door walks his most—or perhaps only—competent co-worker, Laura Dintly. She looks the situation over, tilts her head as if to ask, 'need a hand there, friend?' and shoots a warm smile. Ivan smiles back. A grave mistake.

The elderly woman looks past her shoulder at the woman in uniform behind her. A frown creases her face while she snaps her fingers in front of Ivan, reacquiring his attention.

Laura walks to her desk briskly and sets herself to work.

"I haven't even gotten to the worst part. At the grocery store, he *found* me, and he yelled at me! He threatened me. This man is a psychopath. I'm concerned for my safety!"

"I understand, ma'am. I just need you to relax for a moment. We'll look into it. Nothing bad is going to happen to you. Was this at Coffee Stop Station? And you got groceries at Prair Pass Grocer, is that correct? Do you have any more information on the man?"

She gives an angrily detailed description. Ivan writes it all down, although it's mostly average stuff, Ivan should easily be able to pinpoint the guy. He makes a note to begin by checking out the coffee roasters and the grocery store.

Ivan grabs his jacket and heads for the door, shooting Larry's gaze down with a dirty look. It's hard to feel anything ill towards the guy Ivan's looking for. If he's being completely honest with himself, he really wanted to dump coffee on the woman at a couple points in their discussion. But she's just a bitter old lady.

All in a day's work, I suppose, Ivan thinks as he leaves the building.

* * *

*Laura*

She'd always been a fan of fictional depictions of the hard ass detective. The grizzled, scarred up face, the cigarette hanging precariously from the corner of the mouth, the mysterious backstory that's never fully fleshed out. It intrigued her. More than that, and she would never admit it to anybody, in certain ways it actually *inspired* her.

Laura imagined working with that kind of cop, or being that kind of cop, while she shifted papers into neat little piles on her desk

and then transferred those neat little piles to their own folders. To be    41
organized is to be professional, her father always used to say.

Used to. She still hadn't gotten used to thinking of it like that.
Her parents *used to* be alive. They *used to* tell her stories about their
time on the force. They *used to* make her and her brother, Benny,
pancakes every Sunday. They used to do a lot of things.

A tear crept to the corner of her eye without her noticing. She
shut her eyes, hard and forced those thoughts out. She reminded
herself to call Benny this evening, or this weekend if she was too
tired, or next week if she was too busy.

The closest thing she got to the hard-boiled detective in her
department would also be the most outwardly bitter man she'd
ever met. Ivan had worked the force since long before she'd started.
Probably since before she'd even passed her entrance exam. He
looked it, anyhow. The work hadn't been kind to him, or he hadn't
been kind to himself because of the work.

Most people aren't cut out to be officers of the law, while some
few are. Fewer still are so damn good at being cops that they don't
have any other option, even if they hate it, and it's not all that good
for them. Laura imagined Ivan to be that type, although she wouldn't
put it past herself to romanticize the idea of him a bit. Being the
only one in her department that seemed to put in an honest day's
work, every day, made him stick out to her.

Laura took her seat at the desk she'd been occupying from Monday
to Saturday for the last three years, eight months, and twelve days.
To the left of her were three desks separated by twelve-inch-high
walls of particleboard. Two of the occupants of this desk trifecta had
never exchanged more than ten sentences with her. She knew their
names to be Richard and Monica, though she had never seen them
leave their desks or do any real police work. The third happened to
be a grotesque beast of a man named Larry. He had spoken to her
quite a lot, although she'd taken to avoiding the response. Most of
what he said was blatant sexual harassment. At first, she'd challenged

it, trying to use her obvious advantages in both height and strength to shoot down his advances. Standing close to six feet tall, which was several inches taller than Larry could claim, and having a body fat percentage around twenty, Laura could easily stand over the man and insinuate her strength. This had no effect whatsoever. If anything, it seemed to encourage him. Laura was fully aware that she could physically ruin the man with three simple movements—grabbing his waggling pointer finger, twisting his elbow under the weight of his body, and giving one hard kick to the back of his knee—but she would never do that. They were *supposed* to be on the same team.

So, she took to ignoring him. This had worked vastly better than anything else. Nowadays she would get nothing worse than a vile wink of his eye any time she failed to avoid eye contact. That she could deal with. Besides, it wasn't often that she was at her desk. Even when she had deskwork to do, she'd taken a liking to doing it in her cruiser in some desolate parking lot.

Laura had only come in today in order to pick up the case notes that had sat in the bottom drawer of her desk since her first month on the job.

*Nola Kemping. Missing.*
*Address: #4 Range Road 19, Prair County*
*Suspects: Joe Shill (dismissed)*
*Witnesses:*
*Family:*

It was the vaguest page in her entire notebook. The only reason anybody noticed Nola missing was her cows showing up at the fence of her neighbor's farm, mooing hungrily and pawing at the dirt under their barbed wire fence.

"Nola never mistreated them animals. They barely wandered ten feet from her house. More like house dogs than farm animals," David Duggery had said.

His time on the suspect list lasted all of twenty-five minutes before seven different people at the local pub supported his alibi. David was the only person who seemed to be broken up about it, he'd make a point of pulling Laura aside every time he saw her just to ask if she'd made any progress on the case.

It broke her heart to have to tell him no every single time.

She let her eyes wander over the mostly blank page for the thousandth time, not even really looking at it anymore. Every once in a while, a twang of guilt would hit her for not thinking about it. The fact was that some cases just don't get solved. Not many, but some. That's what her father would have told her. She found herself giving the advice to herself that he would have given more and more often. The thoughts even came through in his voice.

It shouldn't fall on her shoulders, the idea of this lonely old woman disappearing never to be found, with no justice served and no questions answered.

Laura rubbed her temples and dropped the near weightless file onto her desk. She looked up to where Ivan was still speaking with the old woman. His shoulders were sunk, his knees bobbing restlessly, his pen hand tapping restlessly against the notepad in front of him.

From her left, an awful choking sound stole her attention. One glance was all it took. When her vision fell on Larry, wiping donut remnants from his mouth, he raised his beady little eyes up to meet hers.

Hello, Laura, his eyes seemed to say. Oh, how I've missed these moments.

She dropped her notebook back into its drawer and stood up from her desk, leaving the building and her coworkers to find something better on the streets.

* * *

His first stop is The Coffee Stop Station, the roasters where Hilleen had her initial encounter with the suspect. Even when Ivan does find the guy, he doesn't quite know what to say or do to him. But he must look into these mundane kinds of things, or else he'd lose his mind.

When Ivan gets through the door, it's a tired, old woman standing at the counter, big coffee roasters working away behind her. The building is essentially a hallway, rows of chairs on either side leading to the counter, their purpose unknown. The walls are brown, counter is brown, floor is brown wood—probably to emulate the color of coffee, although it reminds Ivan of something else entirely. Her hair is in a messy bun on top of her head, and her apron has oily coffee stains all over the front. There are massive bags under her bloodshot eyes. She looks like she hasn't had a good wash in a few days, and her clothes even longer than that.

She notices Ivan and perks up a little bit, going from leaning on her elbows, staring at the counter, to standing straight up and attempting a smile.

"Hiya, Officer. What can I do for you today?" she asks. When Ivan doesn't answer immediately, taking the time to look around for other employees and asserting silence as a sign that it's serious time, she goes on. "We've got the Tuscan Medium roast on special, if you're interested. Ten ninety-nine for a pound."

"Not here for coffee, I'm afraid. Do you have a minute to answer a couple of questions for me?"

He's just gotten to the counter when the smell of gin on her breath becomes almost overwhelming. A twinge of envy pangs Ivan's temple. Envy for her and people like her, working jobs where they can sneak a sip—or in her case a gulp—here and there.

"Yeah. Uh, yes, of course. What's going on?"

"Do you have any employees here that match this description?"

Ivan reaches into the pocket of his leather jacket, pulls out his notepad, and slides a page from it over to her.

"Only person that makes any sense walked out of his shift a while ago and hasn't shown up since. It was weird, totally out of character for him. He's a quiet guy, but always pleasant. Never done anything like that before."

"Done anything like what, exactly?" Ivan asks.

"Well, he *allegedly* dumped coffee beans over some woman's head. She spent nearly an hour in here telling me all about it, shaming me for hiring someone capable of such things. I wouldn't believe it at first. I told her there must be some mistake, but she was very insistent, going on about him being a violent lunatic. Now, I doubt that very much; he wouldn't harm a fly without a reason. But when I phoned him, he totally admitted to it. The coffee bean part, I mean. Nothing violent. Called her an inconsiderate *B-word,* as well, then quit too. A damn shame, really."

Ivan gets his name and address, thanking the woman before turning to leave. Her sigh of relief and return to her slumped position is audible. Ivan has to stifle a giggle.

People's fear of authority can be humorous at times. He can hear a lid being unscrewed from a bottle, and as he pushes through the door, Ivan turns to see her gulping at something under the counter. What a gal.

That was easier than he had hoped it would be. This ordeal probably won't even keep him busy for the rest of the day.

\* \* \*

Well, the nerves are back in full force. The last time I put this much thought into an outfit, I was probably in my twenties. I'm only now noticing how dull of a wardrobe I have. Everything is black, or grey, or a color so faded it hardly registers to the human eye.

I haven't even spent two minutes in front of my mirror and I'm already beginning to bore of it. It's hard not to focus on the flaws— the receding hairline, the paunchy stomach that refuses to flatten no matter how much I exercise, the posture that has always been rather sunken.

Black jeans and a grey shirt. No. Grey slacks and a black shirt. No. Black jeans and a faded blue shirt. Not bad. I'm trying to slip my pants off when the doorbell rings. It's such a foreign sound that I almost fall flat on my face. I pull the pants back on, tuck my shirt in quickly and messily, and rush for the door. I pull it open without looking through the window.

Holy shit.

An officer of the law stands in front of me. Looks like a real hard-ass, too. His hair is clipped short to his skull, which somehow emphasizes his muscular jaw. Over his uniform, he wears a brown leather jacket. There's no sign of friendliness, or any emotion at all, for that matter, on his face. There's a belly hiding under his shirt, but his stature is still strong and built. Not the type of person someone would want to mess with, which I'd guess is precisely the look he's trying to achieve. This should be good.

"Hi there, sir." He pauses and looks over me, clearly noticing what a mess I am. "Got a minute to chat?"

"Uh, yeah. Sorry, I mean 'yes.' Of course. Want to step inside?"

"No. I'm fine here, thanks,"

Well, he hasn't cuffed me yet, so I can only assume this is about the old woman and not the young man from the restaurant. I rub my knuckles, remembering the bruises there. He notices this and stashes it in his mind to use against me later.

"Do you know a woman by the name of Hilleen Credick?" he asks me.

"No, I can't say that I do. May I ask why?" I know why, but I ask anyhow. I read once that with cops it's often best to feign ignorance.

"Look, I'm gonna be straight up with you. You're not under arrest as of right now. This woman has given me an account of what's transpired between you two. If I told you she was short, curly haired, and absolutely bitchy, would that help stimulate your memory?"

Shit, this guy is the real deal. Straight to the point.

"Yeah, that does ring a bell actually. Look, she was being horrible. I didn't cause her any physical harm or anything. I just wanted to give her a little shock."

"You sure did manage that. She's claiming you've threatened her with violence. Is this true?"

I have to think back on that. He takes note of the fact.

"No, I didn't threaten her with violence. The grocery store—I'm assuming that's what you're talking about?"

He nods.

"Look, you're being straight up with me, so I'll do the same for you. She treats the woman who works at the grocery store like absolute garbage. She's awful to her. I've seen it twice now. I simply stepped in and stood up for someone who couldn't do it herself at the time. I basically performed a public service." I say it with some sarcasm that I hope that he picks up on and appreciates.

The cop just stares at me for a bit. I don't do well with the extended eye contact, so I look back down at myself and try to straighten the wrinkles in my shirt.

"Look, guy, I believe you. I talked to the lady; she's no sweet old granny by any means. But you can't go around pulling that kind of shit. It's not up to me if she decides to press charges. Even if you say there was no legitimate threat of violence, she could probably ding you with harassment, maybe even assault." He pauses and looks me up and down again. "But I have to ask, what happened to your knuckles?"

"Oh, that was nothing related. Some guy and me had a bit of a difference of opinion at a bar. He was belligerent, swung a few times before I finally reciprocated." That was the toughest thing I have ever said in my entire life.

"If you say so. Consider this a strong warning. She may still press charges. If I have to talk to you again, it won't be such friendly chit-chat. Just watch yourself, okay?"

I nod and mouth 'thank you.'

He returns the nod. "You should change the shirt. The wrinkles make you look like you don't care enough to iron it."

And then he's gone. Pretty sharp guy. I shut the door and begin unbuttoning my shirt, feeling grateful for not being put into the back of his car.

\* \* \*

*Ivan*

Ivan finds it hard to believe that he just walked away from that man's house. He'd barely made a threat. Back in his prime, he wouldn't have even considered that a warning. It was pretty much just a friendly conversation with the man. Has the slow decline into the same apathy of everyone else in his department begun? Or maybe he is just turning in to a big softy. The guy seemed like a decent human being. Shit, even though he was joking, it's hard not to agree with his 'public service' statement.

It takes a minute for Ivan to decide to start the car and return to the station. He'll need to call the woman and inform her that her account of the threats has been disclaimed, but then he recalls the man saying that a woman working at the grocery store had been involved. If she will agree with his account of the events, Ivan should be able to wrap this up quickly and neatly. He turns the key and gets on his way to the only real grocery store in Prair Pass. Sometimes, small towns just make life easier.

For some strange reason, he just got the gut feeling that man was the kind of person he should trust. Some people have those eyes that make it hard to think they could do anything truly wrong. That guy had those eyes. He's the kind of person whose side Ivan wants to be on.

The accused rolls around in his mind while he drives. More often than he should be able to admit, Ivan wasn't nearly as *there* as he should be while operating a vehicle. He's never once been in an accident, or even written up for reckless driving, though he owed that more so to others' awareness of him than his own talents behind the wheel. At the moment, he was staring down the long stretch of highway leading out of town, not at anything specifically, just allowing his eyes to wander between dry open prairie and dense green mountain. His destination lies ahead to the right. Ivan snaps himself back in to focus, making the turn off the highway, and taking three sharp, quick breaths to wake up his brain.

The grocery store parking lot is moderately full, so Ivan parks far from the doors and takes his time walking towards them. The decision of what to say when inside, and who to say it to, is one made slowly and deliberately. Busy grocery stores don't fall under his list of top-ten favorite places to be.

A manager is not clearly visible, and the customer service desk is a mess of people shouting and employees trying to calm them down. Ivan decides to take a walk past the registers and, more importantly, the people working behind them. Several shoppers shoot a nervous glance his way. Everyone likes to assume the worst; that's something he has learned in his time on the force. They see a guy in uniform and immediately jump to the idea that the place is laden with explosives or a murder suspect was inside. This had never actually been the case.

Often he just grows bored, and hopes that maybe, just maybe, someone will decide to start shooting up the store while he's inside of it. If only he could do some actual, life-on-the-line, hard-boiled police work. Perhaps it would provide some self-validation. Who knows?

Only one female under the age of forty appears to be working, so Ivan takes a shot and walks over to her. She has brown curly hair and a kind sort of face, with a smile that appears more honest than the rest of the employees. He catches her eye, and she stares for a moment before continuing to ring through her customer. Very professional. As soon as she's finished, she apologizes to the next customer in line, turns off the light for her till, and places a "Temporarily Closed" sign on the conveyor belt.

"Officer, how can I help you?" she asks.

"Sorry to bother you at work, I just had a couple of quick questions about an occurrence here recently."

"Of course. Can we step into the break room?"

Ivan nods and follows her quick strides through the produce section into the back. She leads him into a plain rectangular room with one large window to the sunny outside world and a wall covered by two vending machines and a refrigerator. On the opposite wall is one large framed poster of an airplane, but he couldn't venture a guess as to why that would be there. She grabs a water bottle out of the fridge and takes a long drink from it before leaning against one of the three circular tables spaced out evenly through the room.

Ivan smiles at her before beginning.

"I'll cut right to the chase here. Were you witness to a dispute between a man and an elderly woman?"

She hesitates for a moment before nodding. "I was. I hope you don't mind the language, but she was being an absolute bitch. He simply stepped in and told her that it was unacceptable to treat people that way. Something to that effect, anyhow. I'm glad he did, because I was coming pretty close to losing my temper, which likely would not have boded well for my position here."

"At any point were there threats exchanged on either part?" Ivan asks.

"No. I mean, it was a bit heated, but it was clear he had no intentions of violence."

"Excellent. Now, *if* it came down to it, and I truly hope it does not, would you be willing to testify to that in a court of law?"

She nods. "Sure, yeah."

"Thank you very much for your time and your assistance, I appreciate it. Take care now," Ivan says.

He turns to leave, but she raises her voice quickly before he can get out the door.

"Would he get in any sort of trouble for this? I just . . . he's a really nice guy, and I wouldn't want to see him punished for helping me out." She has a hint of red in her cheeks.

The plot thickens.

"At this point, it seems unlikely that any serious charges will be laid. Do you know him on a personal level?" Ivan asks.

"Well, not really that well. Not yet, I guess. We're having dinner tonight, so I guess maybe I will be on a personal level with him after this evening."

Ivan can't help but smile at her. She possesses an endearing quality that he can't quite put his finger on.

"I wouldn't be too concerned, ma'am."

Her face hardens.

"Sorry," he says. "Habit of the job. I wouldn't be too concerned."

"Thank you, Officer. Have a good day."

\* \* \*

The cop was right about switching my shirt. I see a vast improvement after I put on a different blue one, without wrinkles. Vast may be a bit generous, but it's still an improvement. I'm just relieved he was only here about the woman. That is something I can deal with, as I honestly feel I didn't do anything wrong, although maybe slightly outside of the law. Not many people like the idea of shouting at an old lady and dumping coffee beans on her head. But I, for one, stand by the idea that she deserved it. The parking lot incident still stirs up some guilt in my gut, however.

I don't have any doubt that such a douchebag deserved to be hit, but I do have doubts that I was the proper individual to do so.

That visit from the cop has me a bit spooked. I thought my nerves were running high enough just thinking about my impending date, but now I am visibly vibrating and considering just calling off the whole thing. Jill's an understanding person; I'm sure she wouldn't crucify me if I explained what happened. But that probably wouldn't sound all that great. "Sorry, a cop showed up at my house because I yelled at that tiny old woman, and it made me really nervous, so I just shut myself in my bedroom because I couldn't handle life like an adult." No, that just doesn't seem like a fabulous option.

It should be fun, really. I'm sure it will be fun, once I pick her up and things get rolling, but this quickly diminishing period beforehand is not at all enjoyable. I still don't even know where we're going. I'm not used to the idea of doing anything without a plan. There were always strict guidelines, and now everything is just fucking chaos. I have completely lost control of my life. Though the changes in my outfit have made an improvement, seeing my face in the mirror, I realize there's some issues remaining. I've been keeping my hair fairly short since it began to creep backwards on my skull a few years ago, but what little hair I do have is standing straight up. The stubble along my jaw has morphed from the appearance of passably handsome to homeless. A quick shave and a wet comb should fix me right up. I leave my bedroom for the bathroom.

Jill's off work in an hour and a half. I need to find some way to chill out.

* * *

*Jill*

A grocery store can be surprisingly full of gossip. Jill, however, tries to keep out of it, whenever that can be achieved. But being

questioned by a police officer is one of those things that won't allow her to escape the quiet mutters and blatant stares from coworkers. They're mostly little old ladies and stern old men who haven't got much better to do with their time, so one can try to sympathize with them. They need something to keep busy, to help avoid thoughts of their old age and imminent retirement.

While returning to her till, after her conversation with Mr. Police Man Ivan, it's impossible not to notice that the gossip has already begun. Bernice actually stops scanning items and holds up her customers to gloat at Jill's walk of shame.

"What was that all about, *Jilly*?" Bernice's nasally voice calls out.

Jill just shakes her head. "Nothing, Bernie. He just had a couple questions," she yells back without a pause in her step.

"Aaaaaaall right, dear. If you say so," Bernice says, returning her focus to her customer.

Jill gets back to her seat and performs a habitual check of the clock. Forty-eight minutes. Forty-eight minutes to go before she's set free from this place. Forty-eight minutes before her date with a *wanted criminal*. The bad boy thing had never done it for her. Jill never found herself fond of mindless gorillas bashing their chests or revving their motorcycles to try to impress. But he's not really like that. He stood up for her when her employment prevented her from doing so for herself. That's an admirable characteristic in her mind. She doesn't know him well enough to pass judgment on his character, but perhaps that could all change after tonight.

She flicks her till light back on and is immediately approached by a customer with a basket full of cookie dough and eyes redder than the river of blood from *The Ten Commandments*. Jill smiles and begins to ring through his munchies, hoping the rest of her shift goes by quickly.

\* \* \*

**54**  Although punctuality is a trait I'd held myself to fiercely before, it's one of only a few I've made conscious effort to maintain. Decency is something I aim to uphold, and to be punctual is to be decent. At least, that's what I tell myself as I'm slipping on my brown canvas jacket at almost precisely 5:35, giving plenty of time to reach the grocery store and pick up Jill for our date. I retreat to my bedroom one last time to look in the mirror before tucking my feet in to my shoes, taking one slow deep breath, and opening my front door. I jingle my keys around nervously in my right hand while walking to the car. I wiggle the rear view unnecessarily, returning it to its original position before starting the car and pulling away from the curb.

It's a quiet Friday evening in Prair Pass. Everybody must already be where they want to be. I see no activity on my block. Only when I turn right on to the street that will take me straight to the highway do I notice anything abnormal. Two blocks down and to the left, a tall, hooded individual is holding a hockey stick in one hand and wrestling with a car door handle with the other. He's yanking away at the thing, as if by sheer force it will unlock. I've stopped my car in the middle of the intersection. Thinking better of this, I turn on to the street, pull quietly up to the curb a few houses away from the scene, and watch. Then, the car door does, in fact, open. Or more accurately, the handle breaks off in to the hooded figure's hand, and instead of giving up, he smashes the window with one hard bash of his elbow. The streets are quiet, besides the sound of breaking glass. He looks around nervously as he pulls the door open from the inside. I wait for an alarm to sound, to alert everybody on the block that is somehow ignoring this, but it doesn't. The car is a rusted up, dark green wagon that looks older than me. I shouldn't be surprised that it's not making a peep while being broken in to. Things go quiet once again, and in the silence, I decide I've watched this happen for too long.

Then I remind myself of my date, checking the clock I see that only ten minutes have passed. I have fifteen minutes to get to the grocery store. Plenty of time, I'm sure.

I swing open my door, not carefully at all, and I step in to the street. His jeans are black, though they're substantially ripped and made up more of holes than denim, to match his hoodie pulled tight to make a small O around his face. The fabric around his head must muffle his hearing, because he doesn't yet hear me approach. While he had leaned in to the car, he'd rested his hockey stick against the side of it, relinquishing his weapon to rifle through someone else's possessions. An amateur mistake, I'd call that, although I know little about breaking in to cars.

While I'm getting closer, I'm putting more effort in to stepping silently, and noticing more and more how tall and skinny he is. The advantage of a longer reach will definitely be on his side. I creep up right beside him, remove the hockey stick from its resting place against the back door of the wagon, and tap him on the shoulder gently with the handle. He twitches violently, hitting the back of his head against the roof while retracting his body from the interior of the car. I can't help but giggle. Until I see his face.

There's an utter lack of facial hair, and an abundance of pubescent acne. The kid can't be older than sixteen, though he's got to be a few good inches taller than six feet. For the briefest imaginable moment, I imagine myself just handing the hockey stick back to him and walking away, but my reasons for stopping him stand. Breaking into someone's car is a shitty thing to do, whether you're sixteen or sixty.

I jab the hockey stick in to his shoulder, looking in to his blue eyes with what I hope to be a stern parental gaze.

"What the hell do you think you're doing?" I ask him.

"Dunno," he answers, voice muffled by the hoodie.

"'Dunno'? Of course you know." I look down to his hands, where I see a wadded up cigarette pack and a few coins. "For a few cigarettes and some change? Really? Would you say that's worth this mess?"

"Dunno," he says again.

"And pull that damn hoodie away from your face." I say.

He pulls the strings, loosening the hood from around his face, and lowers it off his head to reveal a nervous young boy with a messy mop of curly hair.

"Sorry," he says.

"Alright. That's a good start. Now, let's go apologize to the nice people who live here, shall we?" I nod towards the house we're standing out front of.

"Yeah, I guess," he says.

We turn towards the house together, and as I'm about to drop the kid's hockey stick, he turns on his filthy high top sneakers and begins to run. I'm ready for that. I was sixteen once too, and although I never would have broken in to a car, if I had for some reason, and been caught in the act, I would have run as well. He's only taken one step forward when I hook the curved blade of the hockey stick in front of his behind foot and trip up his lanky legs. It's a long fall for a tall boy, and his face connects with the concrete hard. I can hear his two front teeth connect with the road before he begins to scream.

Shit.

The poor kid didn't deserve that.

He rolls on to his back, howling like a chained dog and clutching his mouth, blood seeping between his fingers. Now I'm the one who wants to turn and run away. His screaming is going to attract attention, it simply has to. Eyes wide with shock and fear, he looks at me from the ground and begins to push himself backwards, away from me. With his hand away from his mouth, I can see that both of his front teeth have cracked and broken, leaving behind jagged stumps.

"Are you okay? I'm sorry, I didn't mean for that to happen," I say.

He opens his mouth to try and respond, but at the attempt to move his tongue, more blood gushes from his mouth. I offer a hand, to help him to his feet, but he recoils from it. Understandably, I guess. But I meant what I said. I didn't want him to get hurt.

Then he stands up on his own and begins to run again. I let him go this time. When he's halfway down the street, I turn in a circle for anybody that had seen what just happened. Amazingly, there's still nobody around. No one had poked their head out the door, or even peeked through a window.

I return to my car, embarrassed and ashamed of myself. What could I possibly have hoped would happen?

\* \* \*

### Jill

Late. Not at all something Jill would have expected him to be. It's only five after six, but even that seems rather peculiar, if she knows him at all. Which she thinks she does. He may not be a type, but he does have predictable characteristics. So, she leaves behind the spot where she had been waiting— just outside the front doors of Prair Pass Grocer— and walks next door to the liquor store. The young man working there flashes a pleasant, familiar grin, and has to turn away when he begins to giggle, likely because he remembers her receiving a door to the face the day before. Jill imagines that to be a hard image to forget quickly. She ignores him and walks over to a tall wooden shelf beside two coolers. Grazing the bottles with her eyes, she selects a red wine with a neat looking label— what appears to be a sketch of an old man's face with splotches of bright colors covering it— and takes it to the counter.

"Ooh, wine time tonight, hey?" the cashier, waggling his eyebrows.

"A girl's got to feel classy," she says, dropping a ten dollar bill and a few coins on the counter and walking out the door.

Just as it's shutting behind her, the car and its passenger she'd been waiting for pulls hurriedly in to the parking lot. He parks in the spot closest to her, and Jill begins to walk over, smiling.

* * *

I pull into the parking lot at fifteen minutes past six. The events transpiring with the kid and the car took less than a half hour, but it felt like several hours. It's difficult to stop hearing the sound of teeth hitting concrete. I tell myself to shut up, over and over again. It's not that easy, of course, but when I see Jill's smiling face bouncing towards me, every thought leaves my head for just a second before rushing back in. She's wearing the same blue shirt and black jeans I always see her wearing, but she has a bag slipped over her shoulder and sturdy brown leather boots. The sunlight shines off her brown curls and brightens her green eyes. I must be a gentleman. I must be something above and beyond myself, take a stab at being something she would want to be with. I can't let anything distract me from being as excellent as I can manage for the rest of the evening. Not even the image of a stupid kid's stupid face connecting with concrete because of my split second decision to trip him.

Before then, I hadn't known how badly I wanted to impress her.

I don't have a plan, but I think I can make that work for me. The plan is to have no plan, to act laid back and go with the flow, be open to her suggestions, and do whatever feels right. It seems suiting, really. My stomach grumbles loudly, but whether it's from nerves or hunger, I can't decide, and I rub it gently before she pops open the passenger side door.

"Hey there, convict," she says before I have a chance to speak.

"Huuuuuhello, uh, what?" I ask. How could she already know?

"An officer of the law came by the store today to ask me about our little situation with that old witch the other day. Have you met him yet?"

Shit. I'm almost glad that she's referring to the woman, at least relieved she doesn't yet know about what happened not even an hour ago.

"Oh, damn it. Yeah, he came by my house. Shit. I'm really sorry. He came *here*? But why?" My frustration is obvious, so she waves her hands in my face.

"Don't be sorry. I'm just glad everything is okay. Everything *is* okay, right?"

I hesitate for a moment, wanting so badly to just tell her the reason for the bruises on my knuckles, or what kind of noise is made by a teenage kid's teeth hitting pavement, but it seems too early to delve into something so dark. Instead, I tuck my hands in to the sleeves of my jacket and put on what I hope to be a reassuring smile.

"Things are fine, yeah. No need to worry. The guy was understanding. Said he talked to the lady and agreed that she's a bit of a bag. She could still press charges though, so I guess we'll see."

She still seems concerned, so I wave my hands in her face much in the same manner as she had in mine, making sure she can see only my palms. But I know I can't hide the bruises forever.

"Don't worry about it. So, where do you wanna go?"

She pauses and has to put effort into removing the worry from her face.

"I don't know. I had a weird day. I'm pretty hungry. Food?" she asks, suddenly back to her usual self.

I smile and nod before starting the car and pulling out of the parking lot.

Things with Jill just seem so easy; it's hard for me to have much of a care about anything outside of the moment.

\* \* \*

*Ivan*

What a day. Not a lot goes on around the town of Prair Pass. Already the police have seen the old lady in with her complaints, and now walks in some asshole in a leather jacket with a pretty purpled up face. He looks around the station with obvious entitlement, disgusted that nobody is yet helping him. Ivan joins him in looking around the place for a moment before letting out a breath and getting up to approach him.

"Yeah, I wanna report some asshole who beat the hell out of me in a parking lot." He starts telling Ivan the story before he's even reached the front desk. It's a challenge not to laugh at him.

"Okay. What exactly happened?" Ivan asks.

"I just fuckin' told you, man. Guy came out of nowhere in a dark parking lot. Beat my face pretty good. Right outside of a sushi joint downtown. Got in me and my girl's business for no good reason. I woulda hit the guy back, but he was an old man, and I don't hit old guys. He was a spry old bastard though." He finishes and takes a sharp breath, almost asking Ivan to express any doubt in his story.

"Just a minute. We'll get you set up to give us a description and a full statement. Would you like to sit down? Coffee or anything?" Ivan does his best to sound pleasant and supportive.

"Nah, I don't need nothin'. Let's just get this done with."

Impatient little shit. Ivan returns to his desk to retrieve some paperwork, and only then did things begin to connect themselves in his mind.

The old lady. The man. The bruised knuckles. Shit. Ivan really wanted him to get off okay, but it's rather difficult to see that happening now. It would be shirking his duty not to connect the dots and arrest the man on assault charges.

For now, Ivan supposes it's best to feign ignorance, to ask the guy in the leather jacket the normal questions and get whatever information from him that he can manage. It would be wrong to make assumptions, anyhow. That's not what good cops do. And Ivan still wants to be a good cop.

"Okay, so let's start from the beginning. Whereabouts were you when this took place?"

The man gives his full account, and Ivan doesn't say a word. He describes the guy perfectly; he tells him that he was a pretty damn average sort of man.

A lot of what comes out of this kid's mouth pisses Ivan off. He thought he just looked and spoke like an asshole at first, but it's so much more than that. His arrogance is seeping out of him like sweat, dripping from his words. Over and over he refers to his "girl" and how she was good until that night. It sounds more like he's talking about a pet than a significant other.

But Ivan nods supportively, making brief notes, and trying his best to look like he gives a damn about the brat's injuries.

"To top it all off, that old bastard took my girl with him when he left," he finishes.

Well, that's an interesting twist. Everything else was pretty much what Ivan expected, but that closing line certainly sticks out.

He makes an actual note before looking him over once more, as if to say "Anything else?"

He stares back with one big, stupid eye, the other too swollen to get a good look at.

"Do you want me to get someone to take a look at that? Looks pretty nasty," Ivan asks.

"Nah. I'm fuckin' fine. Just find that guy and get the damn old loony off the streets," he orders.

Ivan nods and closes the report, taking it back to his desk. It had been a long day already, and he's in no mood to deal with this.

\* \* \*

*Laura*

Her cruiser sat in her driveway, the lights off, the engine cooled almost completely. It was quiet. She enjoys the quiet. She could get some thinking done without the constant clicking of keyboards and groaning of fellow officers. Her notebook sat open in her lap, a cup of lukewarm, black coffee sitting in her cup holder.

"Where did you go?" Laura whispered to the page in front of her. Unanswered questions were a sign of failure in her line of work, and she couldn't stand failure.

Her radio crackled, a brief glimmer of hope for something to do, before going silent again.

Max would lose his mind entirely when she walked through her front door. The second her key entered the lock, she would hear his tail rapidly sweeping the laminate floor inside. He would let out one low bark before recovering his cool and quieting down. When she walked in and smiled down at her boy, saying, "Hullo, Max! How's my little boy doing?" his entire body would wiggle back and forth, driven by the sheer force of his tail. He would begin to squat down, preparing to jump up on her before remembering that he's not allowed.

Max's large, square head would find a comfortable place between her knees until Laura knelt to give him pets and accept his kisses. His brindle coat would shine under the kitchen lights, and his big, goofy smile never failed to make her laugh.

Her brother told her to be careful when she told him she'd adopted a pit bull. He told her that they're strong, stubborn, and mean. She came to find those words were three of the last she would use to describe Max.

But today, when she got out of her car and walked up to her house, giddy as the first day she brought her pup home, something was different. When she inserted her key, there was no rapid sweeping from the other side of the door.

* * *

I drive around aimlessly while Jill and I make small talk. Eventually, I ask her what she'd like to eat. I expect, for a moment, for her to respond passively. "Whatever you'd like is fine." But that's not even close to the way she is.

"I'm in need of something with noodles, if that's fine by you. I've had a mean ramen craving for like, three weeks now. But Italian or Chinese would be alright with me as well," she says.

I smile and look to her face, where there is no sign of sarcasm.

"That sounds great to me. I actually know a pretty good little place," I say, taking a turn towards the only Japanese restaurant I know.

We drive in silence for a while. Somehow, though, it's the type that doesn't feel uncomfortable or awkward. It doesn't demand to be filled with banter. I haven't felt that with anybody since Debbie died. But there they are again, those thoughts and feelings I don't want to feel.

Arrival at Tengoku Sushi is quick, as I was subconsciously heading there before Jill said anything. Perhaps we'll have an encounter with my latest victim. Wouldn't that just be *thrilling*. I park exactly where his car was parked that night, and laugh quietly to myself. Jill looks over at me and tilts her head as if to ask me why I'm laughing. I just shake my head. "Shall we?"

I'm glad to see, as we approach on foot, there is only one couple waiting between the first set of doors and the second. Jill looks over their shoulders a bit anxiously, and my stomach rumbles in agreement with her impatience.

"Do you want to go somewhere else?" I ask.

"I don't know. Now that I've got the idea of Japanese food in my mind and the smell is hitting me, I don't think anything else will be satisfying. Is it okay if we wait?"

"Yeah, absolutely," I say.

I'm happy with her decision. I think I'd be happy with whatever she decided, though. If I'm being totally honest, I'm perfectly indifferent towards where we go or what we do. While she's around, I just don't worry about that kind of thing. I'd go where she wants to go and do what she wants to do.

Jesus, listen to me, I'm smitten like a schoolboy. I can't even feel any shame about it, although that will probably surface later on. I'm just enjoying myself too much.

"You're not much of a talker, are you?" she asks.

Uh oh. Here it comes. The "What's wrong? Why are you so quiet? Do you not want to talk to me? Should I go?" that always comes up when I try to get close to someone.

"I'm sorry, really. It's nothing to do with you. I'm just quiet, I guess. I'm sorry," I say.

"Hey, no. Don't apologize. I kind of like it," she says. "Not that I don't want you to talk. I want to get to know you. But doing that slowly, with silence in between, is totally fine by me. I'd rather not talk about anything neither of us cares about."

God. Damn. As if her allure wasn't already topped out. All I can do is smile.

"Thank you," I say. "That's wildly relieving."

She smiles back and we continue to wait in silence, looking around at people slurping up noodles or struggling to fit a larger piece of sushi in their mouths. I can't help but look at her as she's looking around. Her pale skin glows softly under the lights as she gently sways back and forth.

\* \* \*

*Ivan*

Ivan's stomach groans unhappily, letting him know that he's hungrier than hell and that he needs to get away from his stupid desk in his stupid station filled with stupid cops. The obnoxious assholes are all sitting around in a circle at Larry's desk pod talking about getting loaded later, and Ivan can't handle it any more. He grabs his jacket and stomps out the door with it hung over his arm, flipping them

off under cover of his coat. It's a small gesture that nobody else will know about it, but it makes him feel a bit better.

The restaurant where the reported assault occurred is conveniently close, though in a town this size, most things are. Ivan decides to kill two birds with one stone and grab some dinner there while doing some questioning. He's not even huge on Japanese food, but maybe they'll have some of that tasty deep-fried shit that he likes.

It's going to be a nice night tonight, Ivan can already tell. The sun is far from setting, but the clouds are already turning that calming purpley-pink color. Good night to make an arrest. See, in Ivan's years at the police department, he's developed this theory that the sky will decide how a perpetrator will act when being handcuffed. If it's cloudy, they'll be pissy and mouth off at you, but they won't physically react too terribly. If it's raining, they'll try to wiggle and spit on you a bit, but they won't throw any punches. What you really have to look out for is the full moon. Ivan is no sort of superstitious goof, but if a cop can avoid making an arrest on a full moon, they should do it. Those bastards will punch and kick and bite like a donkey. They'll do anything in their power to hurt you and keep those cuffs off. He's never fired his weapon at someone with the intent of killing them, but the closest he's come was on a Halloween night with a big, beautiful, full moon. It just puts those crazies into a trance. They feed off it.

He's never had trouble on a night like this, and he's hoping to keep it that way.

\* \* \*

It didn't take all that long for us to get a table. When asked what we would like to drink, I look at Jill blankly and she smiles between the drink menu and me. She asks if I feel like a glass of wine, and when I agree, she orders something for the both of us. Something with a fancy name in a language I couldn't put my finger on.

While I'm browsing the menu, she raises her eyes to my hands, and more specifically, my right hand, the one covered in bruises. I catch her staring and she quickly returns her eyes to her menu before a thought crosses behind her eyes, and she meets my gaze confidently.

"Those bruises," she begins, "is that why you were late to pick me up, by any chance? Not that I mind. The lateness, I mean. It just seems a bit odd for you. And if you're out getting in fist fights on a regular basis, I feel like that's something I deserve to know sooner rather than later."

I shouldn't have tried to avoid it. I should have just told her what happened straight away.

"I'm sorry I was late, that's definitely not like me. The bruises aren't related. I got caught up with something and lost track of time. And I promise, I'm not a big fighter, this was a rare occurrence." I hold up my hand guiltily.

She takes some time looking between my hand and my face, trying to decide if she believes me or not. I contemplate continuing my admission of guilt, telling her about why I was actually late, but I decide that can wait.

After several long seconds, she claps her hands together in her lap, and chews on her bottom lip before speaking.

"I'm going to believe you. Generally, at least I think, I'm a pretty good judge of character. I want to trust you, so I'm going to. But if there is a next time for something like this," she waves her hands around mine, "don't try to hide it. Deal?"

I nod my head and smile, glad to have that matter behind us.

We spend more time looking around and watching others interact than we do actually interacting with one another. It's beginning to make me question if we'll have anything in common. As soon as it starts to grow into a serious concern, Jill interrupts my train of thought.

"So, what do you do? I don't mean for work or whatever, although I'm curious about that too. But, what do you enjoy doing?"

"Hah, well, I can't say I have a serious list of hobbies. My list of employment is even shorter, though." Oh, aren't I charming? "Uh, I used to roast coffee beans. It was nice, easy, and paid surprisingly well, but it just couldn't last forever, you know? I guess you could say I'm between jobs right now."

"Okay, so, what about the other stuff? The hobbies? The *juicy* stuff, come on!"

She seems actually interested in what I do with my time. It's refreshing to speak to someone who listens rather than just waiting for their turn to speak.

"Don't get too excited! I'm honestly quite boring. I read a lot. I used to do a lot of running. I dunno. Nothing out of the ordinary, I guess."

"Oh, come *on*," she urges. "There's got to be more to you than that."

I reach out mentally for something, anything about myself that could interest her. Oh, yeah! How about the thing where I beat the hell out of some guy in the very parking lot of this restaurant! That's got to be appealing in some way, right?

"I'm just not that interesting, I suppose."

"Alright, alright, you keep your guards up. I'll get in there eventually," she says. Her glass of wine has drained rather quickly, and she's having no issue running this conversation.

I laugh honestly with her.

"I'm sure you will, Jill. Now, what about you? What do you do outside of being the best damn Prair Pass Grocer employee ever?" Look at me, getting all personal. My wine must be helping my cause as well.

"Well," she starts, before something terrible happens to interrupt her.

In through the door walks mister police man, the same I talked to earlier, and both mine and Jill's jaws drop and quiver just a little bit. Did the woman decide to press charges? Am I about to be arrested in the middle of a nice restaurant, whilst on a first date? Could anything more humiliating happen?

Although we both see him and he surely sees us, it seems like he pretends not to. Perhaps he's off duty and simply doesn't want to be involved with anything related to work. Jill looks at me with concern blatant on her face.

"Do you think . . ." she begins.

I just look her in the eyes and shrug while shaking my head gently.

"I . . . don't know," I tell her.

The officer, Ivan, is seated at the sushi bar and doesn't even take a single glance at us.

"Do you want to go? I'll totally understand if you do," Jill says.

"No, absolutely not. I'm having a nice time," I say.

She smiles at me and nods.

The waitress finally returns and we place our order. Jill asks me to share something, and I agree with half my mind still elsewhere. I barely know what I agreed to. I just keep hoping that I can walk out of here after dinner without handcuffs on my wrists.

\* \* \*

*Ivan*

Ivan saw him. Of course, he saw him. Of course, the fool comes back here. He takes his date to the place that he "reportedly" beat the hell out of some young asshole. Why couldn't he have just gone somewhere else? He can only pretend not to see him for so long. Ivan's already ordered and is sipping some cheap whisky, trying to lose his ability to think about the man he should be questioning. He'll ask his questions after he's eaten, as he's technically not on the clock right now. He can only hope that they will be gone by then, and that he won't have to interrupt what looks to be like a nice evening.

\* \* \*

It's hard to grasp, but I think the presence of that cop is a coincidence. He hasn't even batted an eye in our direction, so I feel like I may be in the clear. I start to loosen up again, and put my focus back into the conversation that has died down drastically since his entrance.

Jill is sharing details from the life of a Prair Pass Grocer employee, explaining the history of the longest standing grocery store in town, with little enthusiasm but no bitterness, when our food arrives at the table. I'd forgotten what I ordered, but now that I see the plate full of sushi rolls and the giant bowl of noodles placed between us, my stomach begins to rumble. A sly smile crosses Jill's face, and she says something quietly under her breath.

"What's that?" I ask

"Oh, doesn't this just look great? I'm starving."

I appreciate her excitement. It makes me feel better about everything.

She hesitates, looking at me to make sure what she's about to do won't offend me, then uses her fingers to pop a piece of sushi in her mouth. I smile and do the same, then wash it down with a sip of wine and take a closer look at the noodles. Broccoli, green onions, bean sprouts, and quartered, soft-boiled eggs are swimming in the broth. It smells fantastic.

"Do you mind if I try a bite of this?" I ask. "It smells way too good."

"Of course! We're sharing it. Do you really think I could eat all of that myself?" She laughs slowly, but then pauses and grows serious. "Actually, yeah, I probably could. But I guess we can still share."

I slurp up some noodles and feel a small part of myself float out of my body in pure joy. Jill is eyeing me curiously as I chew and swallow. Apparently, my face tells the story of what just happened in my mouth.

"That good, huh?" she asks, before grabbing her chopsticks and slurping some up for herself.

"It's amazing," I tell her.

She nods violently while chewing, and I can tell she's on the exact same page.

"I'm so glad you're here," I begin, before realizing that's a bit cheesy and may be pushing the boundaries a bit. "Or, you know, I never would have ended up ordering these noodles," I finish awkwardly.

"Hah, so that's all I'm good for, hey? Finding the good noodles for you. I see how it is," she says, deadpan.

"No, that's not what I meant. I promise!" My cheeks burn with embarrassment.

"I'm just messing with you! Don't worry, I know what you meant." I swear I can see some red coming to the surface of her cheeks as well, even if she covers it up quickly by taking a drink of wine.

I think this is going quite well.

"You know, I'm really enjoying myself. Thanks for asking me to do this," she says, and now it's my turn, again, to feel the blood rush to my face.

"I am too," is all I can manage to say. The rest of my thoughts I try to convey with a smirk.

We continue to eat and drink until the food and wine is gone and we both feel sleep creeping on. My body feels heavy and my eyes feel warm. The bill comes and it is placed directly in the middle of the table. We both reach for it at the same time.

"Please, allow me," I say.

"No. Please, allow *me*," Jill says.

"I wouldn't feel like much of a gentleman if I let you pay for dinner," I tell her.

"You invited me, you picked me up, and I genuinely enjoyed myself," she says.

"But this was my idea. That means I should pay, I think,"

"How about this," she says. "I'll take care of it this time, and next time you can?"

"So, there will be a next time?"

She grins and nods.

"Okay. I guess I can live with that," I say.

She pays for our dinner, and as we're heading for the door, she gives my hand a gentle squeeze.

\* \* \*

*Ivan*

Finally, they've headed for the door. Ivan finished eating long ago, and he could very well be on his seventh whisky. It's starting to lose its burn, and he'll certainly be in no shape to drive any time soon. He remembers, briefly, that he has a job to do here. He'll have to pretend to be a bit more sober than he is. Having a belligerently intoxicated cop asking questions in a peaceful establishment such as this will not look good.

The sushi chef has been glancing over nervously for the past five or ten minutes. Ivan's been keeping his eyes mostly on his drink. He can tell it's about time that he gets out of here. He flags down his waitress rather rudely and asks for his bill, simultaneously pulling out a shiny piece of officer identification. When she returns, he shows his badge and asks if he could ask her a couple of questions in a slightly more private place. She looks frightened. He tries to assure her there's nothing to worry about, that he's just following up about an occurrence in the parking lot. She says something under her breath that he doesn't quite manage to catch and begins to walk towards the back, turning and motioning for him to follow. Ivan finishes his drink, shudders slightly, and goes after her.

There's a small office in the back behind the kitchen, walls lined with heavy filing cabinets and a computer desk in the corner farthest from the door, where she leads Ivan. A row of bright, unnatural bulbs along the ceiling fill the room with a headache inducing light. She shuts the door gently and sits down with a quiet sigh.

"So, what has happened?" she asks. Her eyes are a deep hazel, her black hair only a few inches long and swept across her forehead, and although she's quite short, her posture and confidence make her appear much larger.

"An individual reported an assault that took place in your parking lot. Do you know anything about this?"

"We have security cameras in the parking lot. They caught everything. I'm assuming you'll need a copy of the footage?"

"Yes, ma'am, that would be very helpful. Thank you," Ivan says.

She turns her back for a moment to turn on the archaic desktop computer in the corner of the room.

"I know it doesn't matter, but if my opinion did mean anything to you, I'd tell you the guy had it coming," she says. She is still facing the computer, but he can tell by her tone how serious she is. "He comes in here a couple times a month with his lady friend. He always treats her like a misbehaved puppy. Doesn't treat my staff much better either."

"I see. He didn't seem like much of a quality guy when I spoke to him either." Ivan shouldn't have shared that. The whisky has obviously loosened his tongue.

She hands over a CD that she's pulled out of the dusty old disk drive of the dusty computer.

"Thank you very much for your help," Ivan says, before beginning to turn away.

"He was in here tonight. The guy who beat him up," she says under her breath, as if she doesn't want Ivan to know, but feels obligated to tell him.

"I know," he says, and walks away.

* * *

I drove her home. Well, I drove her halfway home. But then she told me she didn't want to go home just yet. She was leaned with her head against the window, looking like she could fall asleep at any moment.

"Do you want to get some sleep?" I ask.

"Not just yet," she says. "I don't drink all that often, so now that we've started, I suppose we should continue."

At that, she pulls a bottle of wine out of her bag.

"Whuh? Where'd that come from?" I ask.

"You're not the only criminal 'round these parts. I stole it from behind the bar," she says, pausing for a reaction. I'm about to give her one when she continues. "Only joking. I bought it at work today, on a bit of a whim I guess, while you were taking your sweet time coming to pick me up. So, should we drink it?"

"You're a little crazy, you know," I tell her. As she begins to look offended, I add, "I mean, in a good way. A fun way."

"So, where would you like to go?" she asks.

"My house is a bit of a mess, but we can go there if you like. I think I've got some wine glasses lying around somewhere."

She looks away from me, out the window, and doesn't say anything. Perhaps I crossed a line.

"Sorry, I didn't mean to be pushy or anything. Where would you like to go?"

"No! No, don't be sorry. I wasn't offended or anything. I just felt like I was going to vomit for a second. I think I ate too much," she says, letting out a respectable belch and then a laugh.

After a moment's waiting to decide, I allow myself to laugh.

She shoots what looks like an attempt at an angry glare in my direction, but by now, I know not to take it too seriously.

"Your house sounds lovely," she says, and so I take two left turns in that direction.

We drive in further silence and take no issue with it at all. We enjoy the company of each other, the very presence of one another, and I cherish it.

*Ivan*

Ivan knows he shouldn't return to the station in his current state. Especially with his conflicted stance on the so-called criminal he's supposed to be pursuing. He's technically not supposed to bring evidence into his home, but he had never been good at the whole "don't take your work home with you" thing. It's sad, but these days, the job is about all he's got.

He likes to think he used to be a pretty alright guy. He genuinely wanted to help people. He doesn't know when he started to lose that—he only noticed when it was gone.

Fuck.

This is that place his mind goes to when he drinks too much. He never wants it to go there, but it always does. It could feel good, every once in a while, just to feel all the anger and sadness and self-loathing that he keeps stashed away all at once. Letting it come crashing down on him like a tidal wave couldn't be the healthiest coping method, but afterwards he tended to feel better. It could be a purging of sorts, although the self-loathing never really went away. It would just hide itself somewhere deep down to come up again later.

Ivan likes to think he's a good cop, but he knows what he's best at, and that is harboring visions of all the bad things that he's been witness to. A better cop would let them go, move ever forward unto a better world. Bleh.

He can't think about work anymore. It would simply be irresponsible. He wouldn't be helping anybody. He needs to go home, make some coffee, and watch some shitty television. Right now, he can't help but be distracted from the road, let his eyes wander off the highway to the houses below, wonder if it would matter much if he just swung the wheels off the road.

Of course, he doesn't, but the thought is there. It used to linger much longer, but these days it will pop in and out of his mind

within a minute. Tough to say if he's just too scared, or if he never really wanted to in the first place. Maybe it's both. He doesn't even know. Home seems a long way away though, and he can't get there quickly enough.

Ivan jabs his pointer finger at the button on the radio and spins it to turn the volume up nice and loud. He doesn't even like music any more, it doesn't mean anything, but it helps to drown things out a bit. The sky is dark and empty and those thoughts come swimming back, so he changes the station to find something louder and slams his foot down on the gas pedal.

* * *

I can't say I'm much of a wine connoisseur, but whatever Jill had stashed in her bag is going down a bit too easily. Upon entering my place, I found glasses and rinsed them out, giving her a quick tour of the kitchen, showed her to the couch, and did a quick tidy up before pouring us each a glass. That is, after I wrestled the bottle open. That was only possible after pulling just about everything else out from my drawers to find my corkscrew.

We've posted up on either side of the couch, and for the first time, things begin to feel awkward. I can't tell if it's been too long without conversation, or if I'm being paranoid, or perhaps there is some weird tension. It just doesn't feel easy right now like it did earlier. I'm self-conscious about my less than pristine home.

I know I have to do something to cut the tension and make things feel less uncomfortable, but right as I'm looking towards her, about to open my mouth, I notice her face in her hands. She is quietly weeping.

There's not a hint of a clue in my mind as to what my next step should be. I'm horribly selfish for thinking in such a way, but her tears are only making my attraction for her grow. I've always been attracted to broken things and broken people, not because I intend to fix them, but because I can relate.

"I . . . is something wrong?" I ask in a near whisper.

For several moments, I'm not sure if she heard me or not. She just keeps sobbing. I reach out and put a hand on her shoulder, trying to be supportive, but feeling more uncomfortable than anything else. She jerks away at first, before settling in under my palm.

"I'm really sorry," she says, hiccoughing and giggling sarcastically. "Probably a shitty first date, huh?"

"No, not at all. It's been lovely. But what's going on? If I can help, I'd like to."

"I'm not really sure. I think I'm just bad at being drunk, is all. I'm supposed to be happy and bubbly and uninhibited, aren't I? Shouldn't I be telling you about my darkest secrets and all that deep gushy stuff right now?"

"I don't really know, to be honest. I'm not that great at it either. To tell you the truth, the last time I got drunk, I turned into a blubbering mess." I don't know why I told her that. I just want her to feel better.

She laughs gently, which makes me feel good, but I can still see the sadness behind her smile. Where there's generally been a brightness in her eyes it's now dark, her nose red and running, the bounce in her curls rather flattened.

"Maybe we could talk about something else? Something distracting. I don't wanna bring us both down. I swear I'm having fun," she says.

"Of course. Absolutely. Yes. Do you do much reading?" I ask, reaching for any topic on which I could hold a conversation.

"Oh, not much anymore. I used to inhale books when I was younger. I don't know why I stopped. Actually, I was admiring your collection while you were opening the wine. It's quite impressive."

"Thank you. It's pretty much all I've got that I'm proud of. I don't know why, I always just found more joy in books than in friends. I was kind of a weird kid. Kind of a weird adult too, I guess."

"Yeah, you are."

I respect how blatant she is. If it was anyone else saying it, I would probably be offended, but somehow, I actually appreciate it.

"Not in a bad way, though," she continues. "You just kind of stick out, while also not sticking out at all, if you know what I mean."

"Thank you. I think." I smile at her.

"Oh, my god!" Jill cries, jumping up and rushing to my bookshelf. "I completely forgot this even existed. I haven't read this since I was a child."

She picks up a tattered, old copy of something. I don't know what at first, until she flips through the pages, first to an illustration of a streetlamp in the middle of a snowy forest, then a group of children tumbling out of a wardrobe.

"My—" She stifles another sob. "My parents used to read this to me. Sorry. Shit. I'm sorry. I probably should have just gone home. They used to read some of it to me almost every night. If they didn't, then I'd cry until they did."

"Hey, it's okay. Tell me about it," I say.

"I don't know!" she shouts. "I just don't know. Fuck. This is not how tonight was supposed to have gone. I'm sorry. I think I should probably just go. I should have gone home directly after dinner. This is my fault. I'm so sorry."

"It's not your fault. Please, don't apologize. Let me drive you home, okay?" I know I shouldn't, with the alcohol slowing my mind and making my limbs heavy, but as I begin to reconsider my offer, she quickly interrupts.

"You're in no shape to be driving anywhere," she snaps, then recoils. "I'm sorry, just . . . you must be at least a little drunk. Shouldn't be driving."

"Yeah, you're totally right, I'm sorry for saying anything. That was stupid. Drunk drivers take lives, I know that better... Want me to call you a cab? Or maybe you could call a friend?"

She chokes back a laugh. "Friend. That's funny. Haven't had one of them in years. At least, not one that would pick me up at whatever time it is."

"Cab, then? I've got a number somewhere." I begin getting up to search around the kitchen, but she grabs my arm before I can walk away.

"Can I—if not, it's fine—but can I maybe just sleep on your couch? I think I just need to sleep. I'm so tired." She sounds ashamed of herself.

"Sure. Yeah, of course." Should I be so immediately trusting? "Just don't murder me in my sleep or anything. Promise?" I say it jokingly, but a tiny part of me hopes that if she does decide she wants to murder me, this will be enough to dissuade her.

At that, she finally begins to act like herself again, laughing loudly, snorting when she runs out of breath.

"I suppose, since you asked nicely, I'll try not to kill you. Just for this evening. Same goes to you, though. Yeah?" She does grow serious, but only briefly. I wouldn't even have noticed if I weren't watching her so intently.

"You've got nothing to worry about. I'll get you some blankets and a better pillow. You get comfortable," I tell her.

I find the situation odd. Trust is an endearing quality, but one that most people simply cannot afford. But I'm not about to kick her out of my house for trusting me not to kill her in her sleep.

I take the best pillow off my bed and wrestle a fleece blanket out of my closet, folding it over my arm and hugging the pillow to my chest and breathing in deeply to make sure there is no obvious stink. The last few nights I've spent on those pillows have not been the greatest, and I would not be surprised if they smelled of sweat and drool. Luckily, though, there is no smell, so I bring them out. She's already fast asleep.

I put the pillow on the couch just above her head, and almost as an automatic response, she reaches up without opening her eyes and pulls it under her face, lifting her head only just enough for the pillow to slide under. I lay the blanket over her gently, and she shies away, trepidation growing over her face, before pulling it up to her chin and continuing to snore quietly.

I smile down at her for one tiny moment before cleaning the glasses off the table, rinsing them in the sink, and heading to bed. I take one look back at her, return to the kitchen, fill a big glass mug full of cold water, and take it out to place on the table in front of her.

When I get to my room, I shut the door quietly, and after one paranoid second of thought, I lock the doorknob. Not because I don't trust her, specifically, but because I've taught myself not to trust anybody too much. I nod gently, assuring myself it was the right thing to do, and I fall onto my springy mattress, crawling slowly up to my single remaining pillow, and falling asleep before I could even think of trying.

My bedroom door is swinging open as if in a gentle breeze, and, even in my mostly-asleep state, I know that I locked it before bed. I know I did. My room is darker than it was when I came in, darker than I remember it ever being. No light comes in through the window. My door opens onto the end of the world, a black abyss where light dares not enter.

Out of the blackness and in through my door walks the last person who could possibly walk into my bedroom. Out of the dark shines a bright light that hurts me, in a way only something beautiful can.

In walks Debbie, like the first day we met. We fell very much in love, quickly, and that was owed largely to the way she could enter a room. She had a way of looking at you that made you feel like she wanted to get to know you. When she spoke to you, you knew she was going to remember your name. She's the only person I've ever met that made me fully understand what it meant for someone to brighten up a room.

But she's dead and gone. She has been for a while. I've been working to accept that for years now. Regardless of whether she's alive or dead, she crosses the room gracefully, beaming at me, and the realization of how much I've struggled to stop missing her comes crashing down on me all at once. I sob, openly and loudly and grotesquely, and she comes to comfort me.

"Oh, my dear. Please stop your tears. Save them; you'll need them all and more before this is done," she whispers in my ear, cradling my head and rocking me back and forth, gently, like a child.

"Y—you're gone. You can't be here," I sputter.

"You invited me, darling," she whispers again, tickling my ear. "I had to come. Just to say goodbye."

"We said goodbye a long, long time ago." I've silenced my tears, upon her request, and manage to sit up straight and say this to her face.

"I know, but it wasn't real. Not until now. You're back, you know. Or you're getting there, at least. I'm so proud of you."

I can't help but smile. The expression of pride was always the single greatest sentiment I'd felt from any one person, especially her.

"I know, or I think I do. I'm getting better," I say.

"You are. You're moving forward, and you're going to do what's right."

I open my mouth to ask her what she means, but she silences me with a kiss. One long kiss that I've yearned for with every fiber of my being for years. I don't fight it for a second. I close my eyes, and she whispers one last thing to me before letting me go.

"It's okay, you know. It's all going to be okay."

I don't entirely remember the dream when I wake up. I know I had it, but it's more like one of those things the mind fabricates only because it wants so badly for it to be true, like an exaggerated childhood memory. I've never dreamed so deeply about her before, it had always been just seeing her in passing, or hearing her voice for a brief moment, something to reach for before waking up, as far as I can remember at least. I guess it just hurt too much. But now I'm starting to be all right again. I'm coming back. Isn't that what she said?

I can feel myself starting to tear up at the thought, but it's different this time. The tears are warm and slow running down my face. They aren't suffocating me. I can breathe slowly and calmly, without gasping for air. I'm not losing control any more. My hands are steady as they wipe the moisture off my face.

That's the kind of goodbye we both needed, whether it was real or not.

I can see her face now, only slightly blurred by the remaining tears. I can see her smiling, and I can feel her rocking me gently as the last memories of the dream come back to me. As soon as they're back, and a smile grows across my face, they begin to fade away again, slowly, letting me cling to them for a short period, before leaving me as I wake.

Then she's gone for good. Or I've let go. Or I've finally started to heal.

Maybe things can feel okay again.

The smell of bacon creeping through my senses brings me to reality. To my knowledge, I've never woken to the smell of food cooking. At first, it frightens me. I run through the scenario quickly in my mind.

Who is in my house? Jill. Okay.

How did she get there? We had a date. It went well—at first. She slept on the couch. Okay.

Why is she making bacon? Because she's a fucking sweetheart and she is cooking breakfast for the both of us. Okay.

Where did the bacon come from? Well, that I don't know. I suppose I should get up and investigate.

I fell asleep fully clothed last night, and although I don't smell very pretty, it would feel rude to get in the shower immediately without saying anything to my guest. I roll myself out of bed, my shirt and jeans wonderfully wrinkled, and give my breath a sniff. It's pretty horrendous. I'll go to the bathroom and brush my teeth before I go out to say good morning. I try to twist the doorknob, but it doesn't budge. I have to spin the lock before pulling it open quietly and creeping down the hall to the bathroom.

Goddamn, the house smells good. I can hear the crackling and sizzling from the hallway, and contemplate abandoning my quest for clean teeth. But my resolve is strong—Jill does not need to experience my morning breath. My only regret is knowing I will have to wait at least a few minutes for the toothpaste taste to dissipate before eating whatever delicious meal lies in the kitchen.

I look myself over in the dirty vanity mirror, and I feel nothing even resembling vanity. I look horrible, like a train hit me and then dragged me behind it for several miles, before wolves picked apart my corpse. It's pretty bad. The bags under my eyes stretch and look like elderly elbow skin while I scrape my toothbrush around my mouth. I rub my eyeballs with some cold water while holding my toothbrush in my mouth and feeling the paste begin to burn at my gums. I finish brushing, spit out a mess of white foam and blood, and rinse with some Listerine from under the sink. That burns, but my mouth feels nearly fresh afterwards. I slap some color into my cheeks and go to face my houseguest.

I walk into the kitchen to a ball of energy flying around the room with plates and cups and the kettle and frying pans and empty egg cartons and bags of frozen hash browns. The sound of sizzle is much louder in here, to the point of drowning out my thoughts.

"Hellogoodmorninghowdidyousleep?!" The furious ball of culinary passion that is Jill shouts at me.

"Whoooaaaaa, now. What's happening in here?" I ask.

"I'm making breakfast! I had to run down to the corner store to grab some stuff. I hope I didn't wake you up coming in and out. I hope that's okay. Tea? Coffee?" She says this only slightly slower than her opening statement, clearly noticing my confusion. Before I can answer, two hot mugs are being shoved into my hands. "Now, go sit down and relax. Everything will be ready in just a sec."

"Ah, okay. If you say so," I say, taking the two mugs of what I'm assuming are both tea and coffee and heading to the much calmer living room.

I sit and close my eyes for a few seconds to center myself. I take short, gentle sips of the hot coffee, and slowly, the wide variety of noises from the kitchen die down. Finally, I can hear nothing more than the sink filling with hot water, and dishes sinking down into it. Jill rounds the corner, bright red in the face, hair sticking up at random points, and embarrassment in her eyes. She has two plates stacked high with food.

"This is my 'I'm really sorry for getting drunk and being ridiculous and sleeping on your couch' breakfast. I hope you're really, really hungry," she says, putting down the plates. "Full disclosure, don't get used to this. I'm not one to slave over a stove all that often."

I can't help but laugh at her a little bit.

"What? I'm a mess, I know," she says.

"No, no, no. You're really not, not at all."

An awkward pause ensues.

"This looks delicious, Jill. Thank you so much. Really." It does look amazing. She must have been cooking for some time. Stacked three high are fluffy pancakes drizzled lightly in syrup, six pieces of bacon resting on top of three sausages, three perfectly over easy eggs, and a mound of crispy hash browns. I want to continue to thank her, but I'm concerned about how much I'm salivating.

"Oh, just wait," she says, quickly bouncing back to the kitchen and returning with a separate plate full of golden brown toast. "Okay, now dig in."

She takes down a piece of bacon in two bites, closing her eyes and exhaling deeply through her nose. After she's begun cutting into her pancakes, I follow in much the same fashion, stabbing my knife into the yolk of my eggs and letting it spill out. I grab a piece of toast to dip into the yolk while using my other hand to ferry bacon strips towards my mouth.

Between bites, I look up at Jill, and she smiles back with some curiosity in her eyes. It's like she's searching for forgiveness in my face, although I don't think there's anything to forgive.

"This is great," I begin, gulping tea to wash down bits of food still in my mouth, "and you don't have to worry about last night, okay? We don't even have to talk about it, or anything. Unless you want to."

She nods enthusiastically.

"Thank you. Thaaank you. I really just want to forget about the last little bit of the evening, if that's all right with you," she says.

I smile at her and tell her that it's fine. Of course it's fine. A part of me feels better for having seen her in that vulnerable state, even though she's clearly ashamed of it. It's helping me to feel more connected to her, and like I don't have to worry so much about hiding myself away.

We continue to eat in silence, smiling at each other between every few bites. Syrup drips on my chin and Jill laughs at me. Bacon crumbles all over her shirt and I laugh at her in turn. Things are comfortable, and this is the best morning I've had in a long while.

* * *

*Ivan*

Oh, dear mother of some elusive deity. I do not feel okay.

Ivan's first thought occurs between his waking from sleep and the opening of his eyelids. Too many whiskies were had last night, and he definitely shouldn't have driven home. He's just glad he can actually remember the drive. But after walking in the front door, his memory fades. What the hell did he do when he got home? The scent of bourbon seeps out of his pores, and he knows he needs to drag himself to the shower, but he needs just five more minutes with his eyes closed.

Every cop he knows enjoys the act of self-medicating once in a while, but Ivan really liked the idea that he was above all that. Obviously not. He tries telling himself that it's acceptable, because he was doing work while getting heavily intoxicated, but that almost sounds worse. The job and his own bad habits should be kept separate at all times.

"I'm not above the law," he mumbles into his pillow three times before forcing himself fully awake.

He braves the bright light outside the safety of his eyelids and immediately regrets it. Pain pierces through his temples and body. The contents of his stomach roll over each other as he forces himself into a sitting position, rubbing the gunk out of the corners of his eyes and wanting nothing more than just to crawl under the dark, warm blanket and go back to sleep. Ivan takes a glance at the clock just to confirm that that is far from an option. He's running late already and still needs to shower. Not that it honestly matters much. He is one of the few cops that actually show up on time every day. A single slip up wouldn't earn him more than a few confused glances.

Ivan stands up, realizing he managed to undress completely before passing out. That alone is impressive. He looks down and evaluates the gut that's developed, just over the past few years, and tells himself he has to start working out again. He knows it's a lie, but it still makes him feel better.

He makes the mistake of giving his head a shake and has to sit back down for a few seconds. He already has a craving for something horribly unhealthy to eat and a massive soda. He just wants to eat and sleep all day, but he can't. He's a grown-ass man with an important job to do.

He stands back up, remembering that he may have to arrest some-body that he's somehow grown rather fond of. He knows he can't let it slide. He walks out of his bedroom, still naked, and manages to make it to the bathroom and start the shower. The room gets steamy immediately, and as Ivan steps in and lets the scalding water drench him, he begins to feel slightly human again. He brushes his teeth, shampoos his hair, washes his body, and then sits on the floor of the tub to let the water wash over him.

He comes dangerously close to falling asleep and has to turn the water cold for a second to blast himself awake. It almost makes him throw up, but he keeps it down and steps out to towel himself off. It's hard to tell if he has the hangover shakes, if he's shivering from the cold, or if perhaps it's a combination of the two. Either way, he knows he'll be dressing for comfort and warmth today, as opposed to his usual professional attire, though he'll still dawn the leather jacket that he wears every day. His old college sweater with a hole in the armpit is fleecy and soft, and his jogging sweats, which haven't been used for jogging in months, help to warm him up quickly.

He spent too long getting ready and won't have time to make a reasonably healthy breakfast, although part of him knows that it was on purpose. He also knows a fast food place on the way that serves burgers and fries twenty-four seven, and that's going to be his break-fast destination. He might even treat myself to a nice, fat milkshake *and* a nice, bubbly soft drink. Get a little crazy.

Ivan walks out of his room, excited for the meal he's already decided on, to find someone sleeping on his couch. Someone he doesn't recognize. A face he can't recall ever seeing before. He strug-gles to remove his gun from its holster, fingers shaking and fumbling over themselves, takes in a deep breath and, finally managing to get a grip on his weapon, shouts for his unexpected guest to wake up.

"Holy fuckin' shit, man! What's your problem? What are you doing with a fucking gun?" the young man asks.

"What's *my* problem? Who the hell are you, and why are you in my house?" He takes two slow, intentional steps forward as he speaks.

"You seriously don't remember, Ivan?"

Ivan tries to, but he doesn't. As far as he knows, he's never seen this kid before in his entire life.

"We… we killed a man last night. We put his body in your trunk, drove it out east, and set fire to it in a field," the boy says.

"What? What in the hell are you talking about?" Ivan asks, peeking out through his large front window to see his car in the driveway.

The kid begins to laugh.

"Hahaha. You moron, I'm just fucking with you. You really were black-out wasted last night, weren't you?"

"Who are you? Why are you here?" Ivan asks.

"Whoa, all right, just put the gun down okay? I'm Thomas. We met last night at the club, hung out, talked to some pretty girls, and got pretty loaded. You more so than me, apparently."

It doesn't make any sense. The kid's got to be in his twenties. Ivan doesn't even like people his own age; why would he make friends with a little shit like this kid? And he absolutely hates clubs, there's no way he'd have gone to one. But the last thing he remembers is driving home.

Shit.

Did I leave the house again?

I must have.

These thoughts come to him like punches to the gut. This makes him want to walk into work and drop his gun and badge on the chief's desk. She would be ashamed of him. He's ashamed of himself.

While Ivan is having his internal dialogue, his new friend has stood up and moved closer to him. He's taller, with the lean muscle you regularly see on a young man's body—something Ivan hasn't had himself in years. His hair is shaved on both sides, but long on top, a curly mess flopping to one side of his head. A sparse bit of stubble speckles his cheeks.

88 "Sit the fuck back down. I can't remember anything, okay? I think you should just get out," Ivan says.

"Man, I really like you better when you're shitfaced. What is it then? Do you want me to sit down or get out?"

Ivan deliberates.

"Sit down. I still have some questions. But I have to go to work. My head is fucking killing me, and I can't deal with this right now."

Ain't that the truth. His head feels close to exploding, and he can't figure out what his next step should be.

"I feel that. I've got a killer headache too. Wanna get some grub before you go to work?" Thomas asks. "I kinda need a ride home, anyways."

What. The. Fuck. Is happening. Ivan shuts his eyes and rubs them, hard.

"Yeah, sure. You're gonna explain what happened last night on the way."

The kid slept in Ivan's house, and he's still alive, so he supposes he'll have to trust him. Besides, he needs to know what went on last night, after his apparent blackout.

"Burgers?" Thomas asks, reading Ivan's mind and rising to his feet once again with a smile.

"Yeah."

Thomas messes up his hair a bit while Ivan ties his shoes, and Thomas slips on smelly sneakers. Ivan slides on his brown leather jacket. Thomas struggles getting his torso in to a hoodie that is at least a size too small. They walk out the door into the bright and painful morning.

* * *

I took Jill home after breakfast, thanking her a hundred times and telling her that next time, I would cook. She lived out on the edge of town to the east, about as close to the grocery store as you could

get without being on a farm. An underlying feeling of guilt began to surface when I dropped her off, perhaps because I never managed to figure what was bothering her. I want to help, but don't know how, and that's one of the most frustrating feelings of all. Or perhaps I'm feeling bad for not telling the whole truth about the activities I've been taking part in.

The drive home is the slow and meandering type. I have no intention of rushing anywhere. I just drive, and I think, and I recall subtle details from my date with Jill. The way her loose curls of brown hair bounced as she ate, the way she spoke gently but not without confidence, and most of all the way her eyes connected with mine while we talked.

The streets are quiet, and the day is turning out to be quite beautiful. In the center of town, I encounter a few city blocks that have been turned into some sort of market. Roadblocks set up at either side, stalls set up in between, people of all ages selling a wide assortment of goods. I park down the street and make my way towards it, not knowing what I'm looking for.

The smells of garlic and confectioner's sugar, mixing and mingling, is so heavy in the air that I can taste it; the sweet and savory scents pull me more eagerly towards them. At the entrance, a boy of no more than fifteen offers me a smile and a paper pamphlet with a list of vendors and what they're selling. I thank him and take the pamphlet. Apparently, this is something that happens every year in the Prair Pass town centre. Where have I been? I had no idea. I'm in a daze, and the aromas make it impossible to focus my attention on any one thing.

I follow my nose, knowing it won't lead me astray, and end up standing in front of a stall run by a short, round woman with a handkerchief wrapped around her head. Spattering oil all but eliminates all other sounds, and for a moment, there is nothing else in the world but the smell of whatever is being made in front of me.

"You like?" The woman, basically shouting into my face, brings my attention back. She's holding up a stick with plump orbs of crispy dough, sprinkled with brown sugar.

I can't speak, so I just nod enthusiastically. She hands over the skewer and I grab at it like a greedy child. I go to take a bite before noticing the look on her face and recalling only marginally that I'm currently in real life and must pay for what she's given me. I reach deep into my back pocket for my wallet, only to find nothing there. I try to dig deeper, but there's nothing. The other side produces the same results. Panic sets in.

I check my other pockets for something, anything. I turn them out to show that they are empty, and try to hand whatever delicacy she'd given me back over to her. She just shakes her head angrily, back and forth.

"You eat. But you come back to pay later."

"Yes. Thank you." I feel a small, distracting tugging at my pants, just above my knee, "Yes, of course."

I look behind me to see a small girl, barely more than a toddler, and when she stops tugging at my pants, she begins twirling in her flowery dress and looking up at me with big blue innocent eyes. When I finally make eye contact with her, she points at my back pocket, and then off into a crowd of people.

What the little girl is trying to point out to me becomes immediately obvious. A man is trying, desperately, to run away from where I am. He's looking back with a mixture of fear and anger, and he is being slowed down significantly by his dog, a rather dopey-looking, brindle-coated pit bull, which has sat down stubbornly with most of his leash in his mouth. The man tries over and over to tug the dog away, but he clearly will not budge.

When I begin to approach, the man raises his left hand, in which I finally notice a thin bit of a metal rod. I stop altogether, and the man brings the rod down hard on the dog's hindquarters. The previously dopey looking dog leaps into the air and tucks his tail between his legs, shrinking to the smallest size he can before finally obeying his master and following him in a full-on sprint out of the marketplace. I wait a moment before abandoning reason and following them.

A small crowd has gathered at the edge of the roadblock, pointing in what I assume is the direction of the thief and his dog, so I run off in pursuit. When I reach a split in the road and am unsure of which way to go, I hear the poor dog yelp. I veer off to the left, away from the city center and down a dingy alleyway, with tipped-over trash bins and grease stains all over the concrete.

I see the thief and his dog struggling again at the end of the alley. The hope that his dog would turn on him takes root somewhere in my mind, but I can't count on it. I see his arm rise and fall again, and hear the highest yelp yet. Then, to feed my hope, I hear a low, rumbling growl. But the thief raises and drops the steel onto his dog's rear once more, and the growl turns into a defeated whine. They take off running out of my line of sight.

I'm beginning to struggle, but I am not about to give up.

* * *

*Ivan*

Thomas still reeks of alcohol. Ivan almost feels bad for not offering the use of his shower, but he seems to have no issue with it. Ivan was relieved to see that his car was parked outside perfectly, without any damage or sign of inebriated driving. It smells, however, and he'll have to deal with that at some point before getting to work. His fellow police officers probably wouldn't have an issue with his car smelling so strongly of booze, but that doesn't stop Ivan from worrying about it.

"So," he says, "what happened last night?"

"Man, we got wild. You came stumbling into Club Twenty-Two, alone, and bought shots for me and some hottie standing alone at the bar. It was awesome." Thomas begins to tell the story, and Ivan cringes often at how much of a fucking douche the kid is, and how much of an idiot Ivan had managed to be.

Thomas tells Ivan that he bought drinks for him and the girl he became interested in all night, and eventually one of her friends started to hang around. Probably more so for the drinks than the company, but Ivan still feels a tang of guilty pride that a girl at least fifteen years younger was even speaking with him.

He tells Ivan that, at one point, he threatened some poor guy for bumping into one of the girls. Their names, of course, Ivan doesn't remember, and he doubts Thomas does either. Ivan feels like he was dipped in shame and sprinkled with regret.

Thomas shares that they drank until the bar closed. Ivan drove the two of them back to his house, where Thomas slept because he couldn't go back to his parents in that condition. Of-fucking-course he lives with his parents.

"So, Ivan, are we best friends now or what?" Thomas asks.

Ivan can't even manage a response, or to stifle his laughter completely. The kid is funny. It's just a shame he's such a dumbass. Ivan supposes he's just added "That Guy" to his wildly small circle of acquaintances.

"Good, 'cause I already added my number to your phone last night, and yours is in mine, so you can't get away from me," Thomas says.

Ivan looks at him uncomfortably. He doesn't know if he's just old fashioned, but that seems like a rather strange thing to say to somebody. Thomas smiles at him and nods along. They're getting close to the burger joint, and that thought wipes anything else from his mind. His mouth is heavy with saliva, and his stomach is growling obnoxiously. They pull up to the drive-thru speaker and order their food.

For Ivan, a burger with no pickles and extra mayo, twice-fried French fries, a vanilla shake, and a large ginger ale. When he looks over to Thomas, asking him what he wants, he's just staring out the window. He tells Ivan to order him the same, so he does. When they get up to the window to pay, Thomas hands over a credit card.

"You paid for everything last night. I'll get the food," he says, still looking out the window.

Ivan takes it apprehensively and hands it to the woman, who is already impatiently tapping her fake nails on the windowsill. The kid has a strong aura of unemployment, and this meal could be the last of his spending allowance from his parents. But it seems rude to deny him this act of generosity.

"Thanks," Ivan says.

Ivan takes two large bags of food from the woman, passing one over to his passenger, followed by two massive milkshakes, and two only slightly smaller plastic cups of bubbly pop. Ivan thanks the fast food employee graciously and pulls away from the window, finding a parking space, and immediately starting to pull the contents out of the bag. Thomas stabs a straw into his milkshake and takes a long, cold drink. Ivan shoves six fries in his mouth before he opens the box containing his burger.

"Calm down, man," Thomas says. "You're gonna choke."

Thomas has only just taken a small bite of his burger. Ivan can't help but slow down, feeling a little embarrassed. He can't remember the last time he had someone around to place judgment on his eating habits. The kid takes three bites to finish a damned fry.

"You don't have to be so sheepish about it. Eat up. I've gotta be at work like right now," Ivan tells him.

At that, Thomas begins to eat more quickly, but still, he lacks enthusiasm.

Ivan's insides hate him for putting them through such trauma, and although what he's shoving in his face is delicious and it feels right, he knows it will not help him feel any better in the long run. That doesn't stop him from continuing to stuff fries into his mouth three at a time and wash bites down with mouthfuls of thick milkshake.

Ivan starts the car, wiping grease from his lips with a cheap paper napkin, and gets on his way while Thomas is still eating.

"So, kid, where do you live?"

* * *

There, on the pale concrete of the sidewalk, is something that never could have been noticed in the oil stained alleyway, not even if I'd investigated it with a magnifying glass. Droplets of drying blood run up the sidewalk, forming a sort of trail. That piece of shit must have hit his dog much harder than I thought.

I begin to follow the trail. Rage begins to boil in my gut with every bloody foot of pavement. A promise is made, to myself and to the dog, to make sure its owner bleeds twice as much. When I find him.

If I find him.

The blood leads me three blocks straight ahead, and then three more to the left. I look like a mad man: fast walking down the street, bent down, staring at the sidewalk, breathing heavily, fists clenching and unclenching. Luckily, there's nobody around to witness me, at least as far as I know. It ends in front of the entrance to a rundown looking apartment building, the type with a featureless steel door, a bland stainless steel doorknob, and nothing else. Someone has spray painted a crown across the door in bright green.

I pound my fist against the door three times. Not knocking, but punching. Nothing from the other side but silence. At first. Then slow, intentional footsteps echoing, and quieter still, a low defeated whine. Initially, it's hard to tell if the steps are coming or going. When I hear them fall just across the border of the doorway, I prepare to throw all my weight against it and force my way through.

"Hillo?" It sounds muffled through the steel, but I'm ninety-nine percent sure that's the voice of a woman, and not the pickpocket I'm looking for.

"Can I come in?" I ask. I've become the big bad wolf. I'd rather not huff and puff and blow the door down.

"Who are you?"

"I'm looking for someone. He took something from me, and I'd like it back."

"Yes, I think I know who you speak of. He took your dog?"

"My dog? No. Not my dog. He took my wallet. That's not his dog?"

Suddenly, the poor pooch's unwillingness to follow the thief makes sense.

"I've never seen before in my life. Dog does not seem to like him much," she says, finally unbolting the door and opening it a crack to get a look at me. "Why not call police?"

"I prefer to settle things myself, for the most part."

She nods knowingly, looking me up and down. She's younger than I expected. Her voice carried an elderly quality to it, and her back is hunched to match it, but her thin face framed by fiery red hair doesn't look a day over twenty.

"Very well. Come in then." She opens the door all the way and allows me to enter.

When I'm standing right next to her, the full extent of her frail, bent spine becomes clearer.

"Up. Second floor."

She walks away with pained steps.

I didn't need her directions, as the whining of the dog is much louder now that I'm inside, but I'm grateful for her help nonetheless.

The woman who opened the door disappears down the dark hallway ahead without looking back. A single bulb sways gently at the top of the concrete stairs, the light shines on the awful brown paint that's flaking from the walls, it dims and begins to flicker as I take my first step up. A bad omen? Maybe. Probably. Don't give much of a damn. By the time I reach the top of the stairs, I can pinpoint which door will open on who I'm looking for. Four doors down on the right—the only door with light spilling out from underneath. Possibly the only apartment on this floor currently occupied. That would be beneficial.

Do I knock, or just try the knob? Someone bold enough to steal a wallet in the middle of a crowded market may also be bold enough to leave their front door unlocked. I press my ear against the door. I hadn't considered the possibility of roommates until now. The dog has quieted down, only releasing a small whimper every few seconds. The trail of blood had thinned to the point of being nearly impossible to notice. I can only hope that means the injury wasn't serious. I hear no movement on the other side of the door, so I turn the knob a millimeter at a time, not making a peep, holding my breath.

When I feel the door give, I exhale gently and shut my eyes tight, counting to five. I take a gulp of air and push it open, scanning the room quickly. Sat in the corner of the room, chained to an archaic looking heating unit, is the dog, which lets out one low bark in my direction. Aside from that, the place looks empty. It's essentially a single room, separated only by a low wall between where I stand and what I can only assume is the kitchen. One closed door is set into the wall to my right, behind which the sound of running water is barely audible. I return my gaze to the dog, its tail *thwap-thwap*ing on the floor. The momentum of its wagging tail causes its whole body to wiggle, shifting its body weight from side to side. When the dog's weight shifts again, it becomes evident that he's a boy. What else becomes evident is the fact that he's favoring his right side, barely able to put weight on it. The injury is obvious; a swelling, red gash runs up his right haunch.

Yet still, regardless of his injury, and even though I'm a complete stranger, he's looking at me like an old friend. I cross the room lightly, noting a lack of anything even resembling a weapon. When I reach the poor boy, he looks up at me with a shockingly human quality in his eyes, a knowing look that I wouldn't expect from an otherwise goofy looking dog. I begin to unclip his collar from the chain wrapped clumsily around the heater before realizing I need to find his leash if I hope to get him out of here safely. It's only when I begin searching for the leash that I remember why I initially came here. My wallet sits on the tiny kitchen counter, its pathetic contents strewn around. He must have been so disappointed, tearing into his loot to find nothing more than a few receipts, a debit card, and about three dollars in change. The thought brings a smile to my face. But only briefly.

Where there existed sound before, now is only silence. Behind me, from the bathroom, the sound of running water has ceased. Panic sets in quickly. I shove my wallet and debit card into my pocket, not bothering with the other items. The dog senses my panic, struggling to sit upright and letting out a yelp.

"Shut the fuck up out there, pooch!" the thief shouts from the bathroom.

I look around the kitchen desperately for anything I can use to defend myself. I pull open the drawers in search of knives, causing a clattering ruckus.

"What the hell you doing?" His words become louder as he swings the bathroom door open, revealing his completely naked and thoroughly tattooed body. The tattoos look cheap and poorly done, which seems an apt summary of the guy as a whole.

I shove a hand into the drawer and pull out the first thing my fingers encounter. I brandish a wooden spoon in the thug's direction.

"Who the fuck are you, and what are you doing in my place?" he says, not making a single effort to cover himself.

"That's not your dog," is all I can manage, finally summoning some courage and advancing towards the man with the spoon still raised.

"Oh shit," he says. "You the guy I took that wallet off. You a broke ass old man, you know that?"

His slurring speech is obviously intentional, something he's probably spent hours practicing in front of the mirror.

"That I am. Now, I'll be taking my wallet. And the dog. You're going to put some clothes on and allow us to leave peacefully." The dog grumbles agreeably as I sidestep to place myself between him and my thief, who has finally looked down to realize his nudity.

"And what you gonna do if I don't?" he asks, reaching one hand into the bathroom to retrieve a towel, which he proceeds to wrap loosely around his waist.

I look at the wooden spoon, and I look at him.

"You obviously weren't disciplined much as a kid. Do you have any idea how much getting whacked with one of these can hurt?" It's a pretty poor threat, I know that the second it leaves my mouth, but I remain hopeful that the dog and I can leave without incident.

He lunges at me like a snake. I take a defensive swing. He retreats a little bit, grinning.

"Think you a bad ass, old man?" he asks, bobbing from side to side. I don't answer. He lunges forward again and swings with his right hand. Quicker than I thought I was capable of, I bring the spoon down and connect with his arm directly on the joint. The vibrations running up the wood make my knuckles immediately sore. An out of character yelp escapes his mouth as he recoils.

"What the *fuck*, dude?" His tone takes a drastic change from tough as nails street thug to upbraided twelve-year-old in the blink of an eye. It sounds like he's about to cry. Then, he reverts to his clearly forced persona.

"That shit fuckin' hurt. You ain't going nowhere, old man. I will beat your fuckin' ass."

I take a moment to lower the spoon and sigh, underestimating my foe. He lunges forward again, this time connecting with a right hook to my jaw. I stumble backwards, ears ringing from the pain. He laughs obnoxiously. The dog leans down beside me and gives my face a gentle lick. It's a simple gesture of kindness, but it greatly helps me regain my focus.

The thief is still bouncing around laughing when I jam the wooden spoon into his knee. He drops to the floor in front of me, and this time he really does begin to cry. But I don't let that stop me. I rub my jaw tenderly, feeling the bruise already forming, and slam the spoon down on the bridge of his nose. A wet popping noise rings through the apartment as blood spurts down his chest. It shoots out violently enough to reach his towel. That'll be sure to leave a nice stain.

"Ohg my thucking fffgod," he attempts. I raise my arm once more and stare into his eyes, which are now streaming tears down his cheeks. He rolls onto his side and coughs a mouthful of blood onto his kitchen floor.

I take a second to stare in wonder at the amount of blood that can come from a simple broken nose.

"Fust thake deh thucking dog n' fffgo!"

That's all I needed. I don't bother to look for the leash any more. I drop the wooden spoon on the thug's chest and lean down to unhook the dog from his chains. I lift the dog gently, and not without struggle. He licks my face while I carry him out of the apartment. The place has a heavy copper stench in the air, and I'm glad to be getting out.

Although it takes some time with several long breaks, we eventually make it to my car, where I place him lightly in the passenger seat. His injury bled lightly onto my shirt while I carried him, but he didn't let out a single cry. When I finally sit down in my car, although it's only midday, the exhaustion sets in. I close my eyes and rest my head on the steering wheel, taking deep breaths and trying to slow my erratic heart rate. I can't relax for long, and I know that. I need to get this dog to his proper home, or at least a veterinarian, as he's lost a fair amount of blood, but I'd say I succeeded in making his captor bleed a whole lot more. I give the poor boy an affectionate pat on the head while I start my car. He struggles for a moment to lay down; it causes him obvious pain, but he needs the rest even more than I do.

We pull out into the street, and I direct the vehicle towards the highway. The animal shelter is on the outskirts of town past the grocery store, amidst the beginning of the farms to the east. I give his ears a ruffle to spot a blotch of ink inside of his left one. As far as I know, that should be enough to identify him and his owner. The poor pooch should be home before nightfall.

\* \* \*

*Laura*

Max. Oh, Max.

Laura had never shirked her duties as a police officer before. Not once. But her dog had gotten out somehow, poor old Max. She'd searched her house high and low—under the bed, where he would hide during storms, in the corner by the table, where he would sit and blend into the floor while she ate, even back behind the shed, where he got stuck when he was a puppy. Max was nowhere to be found.

The back gate was creaking back and forth, open somehow. He'd gotten out. Max hadn't opened the gate in his entire life, and there would be no reason for him to start now.

She'd spent a long time looking for him, just driving around the city in her cruiser. Laura couldn't even consider it misuse of time; if she'd encountered a crime, then she would have dealt with it, but she didn't. The sun was setting when she finally got the call.

Laura had only ever had to call the shelter once. Well, she didn't have to, but she'd convinced herself she did. She checked their website a few times a week, and when she saw a dog that looked identical to Max, she had to call to ask about adopting him. He was adopted an hour before she called, but their number was still saved in her phone. When it showed up on her caller ID, the feelings

of relief and distress clashed together into something that made her hand shake while she answered.

"Hell…o?" She dragged it out, not certain she wanted to hear what they had to say.

"Hello, ma'am. Does a friendly pup named Max belong to you? We've got him down at the shelter. He's got an injury being taken care of right now, but we think he'll be just fi—"

"Oh, thank god you found him," Laura interrupted. "What kind of injury? Where did you find him? Does he seem scared? I'm on my way there right now."

"Just a minute now. That's a lot of questions. His hind leg has a pretty nasty split that we've been working on cleaning and stitching. He was brought in by a man, although he wished to remain anonymous. Said he picked him up off the highway with his leg already cut up. They seemed reluctant to separate; maybe he's a friend of yours? Max seemed pretty fond, anyway. He's sedated now, but his spirits are high. Our vet never got so many kisses from an injured boy like him."

Laura breathed a sigh of relief. "Thank you. Thank you, so much. I'll be there soon, alright?"

She hung up and turned on the lights and sirens. Her speedometer hit ninety faster than she'd ever imagined possible. She reached the shelter in four minutes.

\* \* \*

*Ivan*

Dropping Thomas off at home, Ivan feels the guilt of allowing him to pay for their meal disappear immediately. The place is a mansion; at least three of Ivan's houses could fit inside of it. At the end of the unnecessarily long driveway is a three-car garage attached to the left side of the house. The double front doors are made of solid wood and bordered by a stone archway. It appears to be three floors tall, with no less than fifteen windows on the front of the house alone. The exterior is covered in stone similar to that of the archway to the front door, creating the appearance of a castle. Thomas notices him ogling the size of it and blushes.

"Nice place, kid," Ivan tells him. "Parents must be pretty loaded?"

"Yeah, they raked in a bunch of cash on their business. Don't like to talk about it much, though." Thomas turns his face back out the window.

"Well, it was nice to meet you. I guess I'll see you around?" Ivan tries to push him out of the car gently, a strong hand on the shoulder applying steady force, until Thomas is squished uncomfortably up against the door. He's not trying to be rude, not exactly. The kid is just failing to take a hint.

"Yeah, thanks for everything. I'll talk to you soon, man. I hope we're all cool." He gives Ivan one short glance before opening the door and hopping out. He jogs to the front door like he doesn't want to be seen by his neighbors.

\* \* \*

In a span of only a few days, I have become like an infatuated teenager. Jill and I haven't been apart for six hours, and I already feel compelled to go see her, to talk to her, to be in her glowing presence. It's weird. I'm feeling that I need to back off, to stop being such a crazy person, but I can't quite help it. I already know that I'd do pretty much anything for her, even if it came at a heavy cost to myself.

Maybe I'm *actually* losing it. Perhaps the unemployment and the depression and the loneliness has finally cracked me, and I'm breaking down more quickly than I ever could have imagined. I'm going to scare off the one good person who has entered my life in the last few years by letting the crazy side win.

But I don't want to be like that, I don't want to be another shell of a person, shambling down the streets with no reason to live but no courage to end it all. I refuse to be that man, so I'll hold it together and calm myself down. I'll force myself to be as sane as I once was, but I'll hold on to the insanity for when it can be used for something greater. I'll sit in my home and wait for somebody to demand my justice, to step in and bring down that hammer—or wooden spoon, whichever is within reach—on the bastards that deserve it.

I know I have to keep my body busy to keep my mind at bay. Already, I'm managing to forget about the events of only a couple hours ago. Within fifteen minutes of carrying the dog into the shelter, they had his owner on the phone. They asked me to stay. In these situations, the owners generally like to say their thanks in person. But I didn't want her thanks. If it weren't for my wallet, I wouldn't have ended up at that apartment. I wouldn't have found the dog, which I learned was named Max, and I wouldn't have broken the hell out of his captor's nose. It was a selfish mission. It shouldn't be rewarded.

The amount my body has declined in such a short time without physical activity is discouraging. My old running shorts are notice-ably tighter around my bloated stomach, but I slip into them and tie my shoes tight, putting on a windbreaker with a zip pocket in front, where I securely stash my keys. I stretch myself out generously on the floor in my kitchen before turning off all the lights and stepping out my door. It's only been a few days since I've gone for a run, but the last thing I want to do is pull a muscle in the middle of the road. I can barely reach past my knees, but that's nothing new. I've never been flexible, regardless of trying and trying.

The first few steps past the bottom of my stairs feel awkward, like I'm stepping too widely or letting my feet point too far outwards, but then my muscles begin to recall that they used to be quite good at this. My feet bounce gently off the pavement, and the aching in my knees is subtle enough not to bother me. I take deep breaths, slowly and with intention. As my heart rate begins to rise, I quicken my pace slowly, challenging myself just enough to sweat, but avoid turning into a gasping mess. I barely notice the cars driving by, their operators glancing at me, which used to be a big issue for me. I used to imagine what terrible things they were thinking about me, but eventually I got past it and learned to focus on my steps and my breathing and not much else.

I run for a while, not paying attention to the passage of time. I run until my armpits are wet and my shins begin to ache in the satisfying way they do after a good run, and then I turn back towards my house and slow myself down to a fast walk. I've run straight up the road from my house, through my often-quiet neighbourhood, towards the city centre and the backdrop of mountains to the west. Four blocks south of me is the highway through town, the main road to anywhere. It's far enough away to drown out the sound of traffic to a dull roar during the daytime hours. I breathe in the scent of pine coming in on a soft breeze and admire the place where I live while leisurely walking back home.

When I reach my street, my pace slows, from a walk to a downright dawdle, not sure if I want to return home just yet. This uncertainty is answered by a welcomed distraction. From across the street I hear a scream muffled by a closed door. My feet come to a complete stop as I listen for what will happen next. I stand on the sidewalk, still as can be, moving only to look around and hope for somebody else to hear what I'm hearing. There's nobody out and about around my house, as I should know to expect. There's another scream, followed by a shout, concluded by a smash.

The front door of the house, an ironically pleasant yellow color, is whipped open and a man spills out, wearing nothing but his underwear, his shoulder length black hair sticking up around his head like he's just stuck a fork in to an electrical socket. He falls down the three concrete steps and lands hard on his elbows, holding his hands above him defensively. Following close behind him is a short young woman in ripped jeans and a black t-shirt, brandishing an aluminum baseball bat. Her blue eyes are wide with an unrestrained rage. I take one final look around for any other witness, and in the house just behind me I find a pair of green, frightened eyes and long brown hair peeking out from behind a curtain. A young girl, only ten or twelve, holding a large cordless phone in her hand, possibly calling her mom and dad, possibly calling the police. When her eyes find mine, she ducks behind the curtain and out of sight while the couple across the street continues to shout.

"Babe, wait! Come on, hold up! Babe!" the skinny, mostly naked man pleads.

"Don't you fucking speak! You've said more than enough. I'm sick of listening." She leans in to him threateningly with the bat as she yells, ready to swing at any second.

*What is wrong with people? First the pair at the restaurant, and now these two. Why be in a relationship with someone you so clearly despise?* I give my head a shake. It's never that simple. And more than that, it's really none of my business, though as it's happening in front of me, and I begin to cross the street, I realize it's about to become very much my business.

I approach slowly, not wanting to seem like a threat, and definitely not wanting to seem like I'm taking a side. They notice me only as a new bout of shouting is about to begin. The man-boy, now backed up on to the lawn and resting on his elbows, has his mouth half open when he looks over at me. The woman noticed me before him, and has taken a step back and let the baseball bat rest on her shoulder. It's clear to me now, from the confidence she has with her weapon, almost as if it's an extension of her arm and not something separate at all, that she's swung it recreationally many times.

"Dude, you've gotta help me, she's insane," the man says from the ground.

"*I'm* insane?" she asks him. "You're pathetic."

"Look," I say, before he's about to retaliate, "I don't know the first thing about what's going on here, but there's a little girl across the street watching all of this unfold. Do you understand me?"

The woman's strong shoulders fall slightly, the shame weighing heavily on her, while the man breathes a sigh of relief.

"So you're saying there's another witness?" he asks.

I can't help but scoff at him.

"Think about somebody other than yourself for a change," the woman says to him, fed up but no longer shouting. "I'm sorry—" she begins again.

"I don't know if I can forg—"

"Not you, dumbass." She spits at the man on the ground.

I find myself both glad I intervened and curious as to how things would have unraveled had I just stood across the street and watched without approaching.

"So, now that we've all calmed down a bit, what's going on here?" I ask, looking back and forth between them.

"He's pushed me around for nearly a year now, and I mean that literally. It's been long enough. Unemployed and sitting around my house, while I pay the rent, buy the groceries, telling me that I'm not working hard enough, that I do nothing for him. I'm done taking his shit."

I nod. After she's finished, I look down to the man who I assume now to be her ex-boyfriend. He's still cowering.

"Well, the little girl across the street was calling somebody," I tell her. "The cops will probably be here soon, or some angry parents. So take it inside."

Turning to leave, the last thing I see is the woman grab both of the man's naked ankles from the ground and begin to pull him towards the door while he whines in protest. The second I'm facing the street, a flash of blue and red lights and a split second of sirens stop all three of us dead. A police car pulls up to the curb, and Ivan steps out of the driver's side with a radio in his hand. He's gone casual today, wearing sweat pants and a crew neck sweater under the leather jacket I've never seen him without.

"I'm going to have to ask you to let his ankles go and put down the baseball bat, ma'am," he says to the woman. I turn to look at her as she lets the ankles fall to the ground roughly and sets the bat down on the steps. Her face is a light crimson, from anger or embarrassment or a combination of the two.

"Yes sir," she says quietly.

"Thank you. What have we got going on here?" Ivan asks. "A frightened young girl called in and said a boy and girl were fighting with baseball bats outside."

When I begin to open my mouth, he finally casts his glance to me and gives me a stern look, telling me to shut up without saying a word.

"She's lost her fuuu—" the man trails off when he looks up at his girlfriend's burning gaze.

"I swung at him a few times, sure, but I didn't actually hit him. Trust me. You'd know if I did. Besides, he's swung more than a few times at me before." She says this in the calm, matter-of-fact tone that one only develops after more than a handful of abusive scenarios. The emotion about it all is something she's learned to set aside. "Funny how you conveniently show up when he's about to get some bruises, but you never showed up for me."

"If that's the case, I am very sorry, ma'am. And what's your involvement, sir?" Ivan turns his attention to me.

"I… I was just walking across the street, came over to see what was going on."

It's obvious to me that we're speaking to one another as if we've never met, but it doesn't seem to be so obvious to the pair on their front steps.

Ivan breathes a tired sigh.

**108**    "I've got another officer on the way. He'll be taking you both in for questioning. You—" he points at me, "will ride with me. I assume you're the only witness besides the little girl?"

I nod.

"All right then. Would you get in the car please, sir?"

I do. Ivan shuts the door behind me, shooting a glare at me in the process.

While he's speaking to the couple, I can't make out words, only muffled voices. Within a few minutes, when their conversation has halted and the two are sitting a few feet apart on the grass separated by Ivan, who stands over them looking back and forth between the two, another police car pulls up to the curb in front of me. When the large officer struggles, but finally succeeds, to get out of the car, I look over at Ivan, who happens to be staring at his shoes, shaking his head. The new cop stands at average height, but holds much more than average girth. His bald head shimmers with sweat in the sun. His uniform appears dirty; grease stains cover the thighs of his wrinkled pants, and the collar of his shirt rolls up over itself. Ivan's clearly not pleased about his showing up, but approaches his coworker anyways. They exchange a few words. The large sweaty one rubs Ivan's shoulders uncomfortably and whispers something to him before they part ways.

When Ivan gets in to the driver's seat in front of me, his hands are shaking on the steering wheel. He watches the other officer directing the pair from the stairs in to the other car, the woman in the back, the man in the front.

"Fuck. Fucking Larry. Why fucking Larry?" he mutters to himself.

I don't pry. He's visibly angry, and I'm hoping that it's directed more at the other police officer than at me, though I can't think of a reason why it would be.

"I don't get you, man," he says to me.

"What do you mean?"

"I should be taking you down to the station right now. They'll be expecting me to bring you in, as I said I'd do." His eyes are red and tired. He actually looks like utter shit, like he was hit by a truck filled with vodka.

"Yeah, I know. So, are you?" I ask, turning the heat onto him.

"I… I don't know yet. Haven't decided. How do you find yourself involved in all this? Just a coincidence?"

I can hear genuine concern in his voice. Either that or an internal struggle of some sort.

"There's some things we need to talk about," he says, actually turning around this time to look directly in my eyes.

He starts the car and begins to drive. I lack the audacity to ask where we're going, though I can't help but notice that when we reach the highway he heads east, where there isn't much else besides the grocery store and a vast expanse of farmland.

* * *

*Jill*

More often than not, when Jill gets called into work, she'll manage to find a way out of it. She got pretty good at making up excuses when she was younger. Playing sick was her specialty. She got to a point where forcing clammy hands and a sweaty forehead on command was no more a challenge than breathing. It was quite impressive, in retrospect.

Today, however, her performance falters. She blames her less than present mindset. She's distracted. He's been distracting her all day, and she can't even be upset about it for a second.

In an act quite outside her nature, she's been humming "You are Always on My Mind" all day.

It's hard to even mind being at work when her mood is this fantastic. She's barely been paying attention to customers, just smiling at them and wishing them a pleasant day. The truth behind her smile must make it rather more infectious than it usually is. Man, to think how much better she could be at her job if she were this happy all the time. Maybe the secret to enjoying life is just that simple. Maybe we're just supposed to fake it until it happens for real.

* * *

*Ivan*

What a day. What a strange day.

Ivan managed to pawn off the domestic issue on Larry, the lazy bastard. It'll be good for him to do a day of real work for once in his meaningless life. But even while doing Ivan a favor, he managed to piss him off by rubbing his shoulders in a mock massage, whispering in his ear and telling him to meet him at the pub later for a round of beers. He doesn't know why exactly he hates Larry so much, just that he does. He knows that Larry gives him that feeling in the pit of his stomach that makes him want to beat the ever-living shit out of him until he can't open his mouth ever again. The way he touches him, the way he speaks, and the way he sweats.

Ivan just doesn't trust him.

But he's played his part and he's helped, to an extent. Now he has to figure out what to do with his passenger. He should be taking him to the station for questioning, but he knows that he won't be doing that, and he thinks the man is starting to catch onto that fact as well. He looked nervous at first, sat in the backseat like a preteen on the way to soccer tryouts, with his running shorts and windbreaker he truly matched the part.. Hell, he looked terrified. Now he's just kind of looking around, taking in the streets.

He's a criminal unlike any other Ivan has seen before. He lacks that look. In fact, when he got a good look at his eyes, he could see empathy there, more than he's seen ever before. He feels trust for him, although he knows he shouldn't—if not for the sake of his personal safety, then for that of his career.

Ivan is not permitted to make personal judgments of character in his line of work. When someone does a bad thing, he takes them down for it. That's just how it goes—or how it's supposed to go.

So, what's so different about this case?

He continues driving, not knowing exactly where he's going to go, but knowing where exactly he's not.

\* \* \*

*Larry*

Larry peers down his sweaty nose at the hard faced woman in the back seat. She has her head against the window. He's shut her in the back, and her boy toy is up in the front with him. He figured she had the bat, so she was the dangerous one out of the two.

He breathes heavily, letting his empty eyes wander over the woman before getting in the car himself.

"Y'all right back there, girly?" he asks, leering through the rear view.

"Fine," she says, noticing his lingering stare in the mirror. "Better, though, if you can manage to keep your eyes to yourself."

He snorts and starts the car. He would've let her off much more easily if she were willing to work with him a bit. Larry didn't have this kind of thing in mind when he signed up for the job. He expected, even hoped for, violence and gory crime scenes. The kind of stuff he'd seen on television as a kid, when his foster parents were out of the house—which was most of the time.

The most excitement he'd seen in his time on the service was getting to point his gun at a kid who'd broken into his ex-girlfriend's house. More exciting than arresting the kid, Larry got to sneak a peek at the girl in her night things. He barely blamed the kid for breaking in, but he had to do his duty and make the arrest, if only to stop her crying.

Now this whole shit show. Damn, was it ever going to be a lot of paperwork for him. He reaches the highway and takes off towards the station, glancing back at the woman every once in a while, trying to avoid her eyes and focus elsewhere. Finishing this quickly shouldn't be too much of a problem. He'd pawn the brunt of it off on someone else so he could get down to the pub for beer and wings. Maybe some of the boys would join him, and he could tell them all about the feisty lady in the back seat.

\* \* \*

*Laura*

The instant she saw him, butt wiggling, tail waggling, and hobbling over to her, she couldn't help but cry. His flank had already been stitched and bandaged, and the shelter's veterinarian said she'd given him enough tranquilizers that he should still be deeply asleep for some time, but he didn't seem bothered by that. His eyes were glazed, albeit lightly, and his range of motion may be decreased temporarily, but Max is still Max. Thank God.

They tried to keep the man who brought Max in around, but he couldn't be swayed to stay. They didn't suspect him of being the one to hurt Laura's dog, as Max seemed quite fond and unafraid of him. She got a description anyways. The vet bill was shocking, and she thanked her lucky stars she'd invested in pet insurance. Max is worth it, of course.

When she finally managed to get him in the car, he refused to stay in his normal spot on the passenger seat. He crawled directly onto her lap and looked up into her face with a pair of big, brown eyes that nobody could hope to say no to. Laura didn't even try to argue. She just started her car and drove home, disregarding her being on the clock.

"There's a steak in the fridge with your name on it, Maxy."

He grinned up at her and gave a gentle lick to her chin before resting his head on her leg.

He fell asleep before they got back home. Laura has to lift him out through the door as she carefully steps out. His seventy pounds feels heavier than it is, being so compacted into his thickly muscled frame. She doesn't struggle with it, though. She's been carrying him to bed every night since he was a puppy.

When she reaches the front door, she has to ease him down to the ground. He whimpers when attempting to put weight on his injured leg. She slides the key into the lock, and his tail begins to sweep back and forth. When she opens the door, he tries to run into the house as he usually would, but he gets only one paw in the door before letting out a cry.

"Max! Please, take it easy," Laura says.

She walks him slowly into the house, right to his bed, where he lay down with a sigh. She steps into her kitchen with every intention of cooking the steak to split with her poor Max, but then her hip begins to light up and vibrate, and when she removes her phone from her pocket, she's reminded that she's still supposed to be working.

"Yes, hello?"

"Laura, we're gonna need you down at the station. Larry's got some paperwork he's probably incapable of dealing with on his own."

There's no waiting for a response. By the time Laura begins to answer, they've already hung up.

"Well, Max, wanna come for a drive?"

He perks his ears up in her direction, but doesn't move. She'll feel bad moving him, but she can't bare the idea of leaving him alone again today.

* * *

Ivan's been driving in circles for a while now. I can tell he wants me not to realize it, but we've been past the same gas station three times, so it's become quite obvious.

He's not taking me in. If he were, he would have done it already. But I don't know what the hell he *is* doing. I've been eyeing him suspiciously through the rear-view mirror for who knows how long. He glances up at me from time to time, but never maintains eye contact. He's a hard man to read, really. There's anger all over his face, but I don't think it's directed at me.

The police station looms to the south somewhere out of sight. I don't think that's in the agenda, however. In fact, as I'm thinking this, we pull into the parking lot of a run-down bar just far enough outside the town centre to avoid attention. There's a small sign above the black front door, "Jimmy's" is written on it in cursive. The bricks covering the outside are supposed to be red, but have become nearly black from a thick layer of dirt. He finds a spot at the back end of the parking lot, where no other cars are parked, and shuts off the vehicle before turning to face me.

My palms are immediately soaked. His face is impossible to glean any information from; it's flat as a lake on a calm day, and his eyes hide everything.

"He came in, the kid you beat up. He wants to press charges. Now, I don't know why exactly, but I feel compelled to help you avoid that. Do you have anything to say for yourself?"

I'd never imagined, before today, that I could experience confusion over which of the two people I'd recently injured. Chances are, though, if it were the kid with the broken teeth, I'd already be in a cell. I breathe deeply once, twice, three times, before beginning to speak. "He deserved it," is all I can manage. I stumble for more words. "He was treating his girlfriend like a poorly behaved dog. He was treating everyone else like shit too. I couldn't just stand by and watch that happen."

Ivan just nods slowly, looking me up and down, not letting anything get past him.

"I don't think you're wrong. I talked to the guy. He seemed like a pretty terrible person. But that doesn't mean I can just let this go.

It's my job," he tells me, shaking his head gently and running a hand over the closely cropped hair covering his skull. He breathes a tired sigh before looking at me and waiting for my response.

"I know that. I understand. I'm not asking for you to let me go or anything. You've got to do your job. But so do I."

"What does that mean, exactly?"

"You have the law to abide by, you see? But I don't. I'm not saying I'm always right. I'm not, and I know that. I'm no hero. I'm no saviour. And I'm no saint. The relative grey area is where my actions lie, whereas yours must always fall in the realm of lawfully righteous."

He doesn't respond, just looks at me quizzically.

"In some ways, it restrains you. The very thing that gives you power, that badge, ties you to responsibility. You're demanded to do what is right in the eyes of the law, but not permitted to do what is right in terms of common decency. That's where I come in, I guess." I say it with such confidence that a hint of admiration glistens behind his eyes. I think I sound like a complete sociopath, but my little speech seems to have done its job.

But perhaps not.

"You're fucking crazy," he states.

I suppose confidence can only take you so far.

"I get what you're saying, okay?" he says. "I do. And I don't completely disagree with you, either. But you're mistaken if you believe I am going to drop my job so someone I barely know can play Justice League on the streets of the town I'm supposed to be keeping safe."

He has a point.

"I don't want to arrest you. I believe in what you're doing. But you need to be smarter about how you're doing it, if you're going to continue," he tells me.

"Okay, you're right, I can deal with that," I say. "So what are we doing here?"

"I haven't got a clue, honestly. I was just driving. I saw the sign and pulled in. I wanted to talk somewhere private. I need to know what you're all about. Didn't wanna just take you to the station," he says, facing forwards again and seeming more relaxed.

That doesn't last, though.

"Shit, what time is it?" he asks, not to me but himself, fumbling for his watch.

"What's the issue?" I ask him.

"I know why I ended up pulling in here. Larry, the other cop I called in earlier to take over with that couple, the big guy, well he told me to meet him here, you know, when he was rubbing my shoulders like a creep. I agreed just to get him out of my face. I was remembering the name of this place in order to avoid it, but ended up pulling in here anyway. Distracted." He's frantically trying to start the car and looking around for anybody he knows.

He's beginning to reverse out of the parking spot, slowly and cautiously, eyes scouting for any sign of who he's looking for. I wouldn't have assumed him to be the cautious type, but I'm seeing him in a completely new light. There's a fear that I never would have expected from him, and I can't figure out what the source of it is. Obviously, the co-worker he's trying to avoid is some special kind of terrible, if he's this desperate to get away.

As luck would have it, the impressively large man, Larry, pulls up beside Ivan's car right as we're about to turn out of the parking lot.

"Ah, shit," Ivan begins to say, cutting off only to fake a smile and a wave to this beast of a man in the car beside us. The fat man is mouthing through his rolled down window, and I can see Ivan considering the option of just not rolling his down and driving away instead. It would be obvious to everyone involved that Ivan is just running away, but he still seems to consider it for longer than he probably should, before reluctantly cranking down his window.

"Where the hell'r you going, Ivan?" the man spits, sweat shining off his forehead.

"I uh, didn't think you were showing up."

"Pah!" His massive belly jiggles. "Course I showed up. Hell, I'm early, ya damn loony. Now, let's get us some cold ones, boys."

I don't think he knows who I am or why I'm in the back seat, and I don't think he cares. I saw him earlier, but he never saw me. He's automatically counted me as part of the group.

Ivan reluctantly begins to reverse towards his parking spot, groaning with irritation. He looks back at me and I feel like tears are about to start streaming down his face.

"Look, I've avoided this guy for a long time now. He's kind of a bastard. Actually, he's a complete shithead. But if I speed off with you in the car now, after he was at the crime scene, I think he'll find it pretty suspicious. That's the last thing either of us needs right now. So I suppose we're playing friends for the evening. You up to it?"

"What's so horrid about him?" I ask. "Besides the sweat."

"I could try to tell you." Ivan completes his park and turns off the car. "But I think it would be easier, for me at least, to just introduce you."

He opens his door and steps out. Then, he opens the back for me. I follow him, lacking any idea of what I'm getting into.

\* \* \*

I look back and forth between Ivan and the beast of a man I've come to know as Larry, thinking that there could not be two more different people in the same profession.

Ivan sits stoic, yet obviously battered and bruised by the job.

Larry lounges against the booth, the button of his pants undone and the zipper threatening to burst apart to end the struggle of holding back his gut. He looks like he hasn't worked a day in his life, aside from the effort it obviously requires to get him out of bed. His pint glass is already empty, while ours haven't been touched. His beady eyes wander the room, searching for something else to consume. His bald head glows with sweat under the lights. I barely know him, and yet I have a feeling in my gut that he's someone I shouldn't be around.

The bar is made up of three circular booths along the left wall, and we sit in the centre one. Ivan got stuck in the middle, between Larry and myself on the outside. The table is small enough that if we leaned forward on our elbows, our noses would be rubbing against each other. In the centre of the room is the U-shaped bar surrounded by wobbly looking barstools. Behind that is what I guess to be the kitchen, as it's the only other door in the place besides the one we came through and the bathrooms, which are against the wall on the right. The walls are painted a dirty looking reddish-brown and largely covered by old posters tacked to the walls and ripped in places. The pot lights dotting the ceiling are painful on the eyes while still not managing to illuminate the place very well.

"S'buddy, who're you, really?" Larry asks me, making the effort to keep his eyes on me for a couple of seconds at least, before continuing to look around for and finally wave dramatically at a waitress.

I don't answer. I don't say anything at all, and he doesn't even seem to notice. He continues waving, shaking the entire table, and threatening to tip over our drinks, until the waitress is standing directly in front of him.

"I need 'nother pint," he says. "N' where's my food at?"

She picks up his empty glass, already over his shit, and begins to walk away. He shouts, "Hey, I'm talkin t'you!"

Ivan looks about ready to strangle him. He actually begins to reach out before the waitress turns around and, in mock politeness, says, "Your food will be right out, sweetheart." She stomps away.

I wish she would just refuse him service so we could leave.

Larry's gaze turns back to me, and as if he thought I had spoken and he'd simply not heard me, he grunts enquiringly. Instead of speaking, my patience growing thin already, I take a long drink from my pint and swallow slowly. I savor the carbonation and the slight burn it makes me feel in my chest.

He gives up on me and turns to Ivan.

"S'how 'bout that broad today, eh Ivan?" he asks, nudging his ribs.

Ivan looks like he'd rather throw up than respond, but he composes himself, for some reason unbeknownst to me.

"Shut the fuck up, Larry," he said. It's playful, but completely serious.

Larry lets out a belly-jiggling laugh, spinning his empty pint glass between his hands.

The food arrives at the best possible time, when the long silence was just about to threaten the three of us with conversation. The family-sized serving of chicken wings and fries is dropped in front of Larry, not by the waitress who had been helping us before, but by a massive, tattooed man with a thinning pony tail. The plate covers the majority of the small table. He's not gentle about dropping it, causing a ramekin of something white to spill over, which Larry seems not to notice.

"Any problems over here, gentlemen?" the tattooed character asks, specifically towards Larry, who has still taken no notice of him whatsoever and has already begun shoving food into his face.

"No problems. I'm sorry if it seemed that way," I say, speaking for the first time since sitting down.

"Keep your buddy in check, got it?" he says to Ivan, walking away without waiting for an answer.

It seems like this is not the first time Larry has acted inappropriately here, and I have no doubt he's used his cop status to get out of trouble at least a few times.

Ivan and I make eye contact and hold a gaze, while in our peripherals, Larry is alternating bites between drumsticks in each hand. We could walk away from the table at this very second, and he wouldn't even realize until every crumb of food was inside his gut. Judging by this glance, that is exactly what Ivan is considering doing.

But our look is broken. Something behind me distracts Ivan, and he whispers something under his breath that I can't quite make out.

I turn around and see a nervous looking young man, far overdressed for a place like this, standing at the front door, surveying the place with anticipation.

"What the fuck," Ivan says.

Larry is still paying no attention.

"Who's that?" I ask

Still staring and wildly confused, Ivan whispers again before I tell him to speak up.

"This guy I . . . met the other night. His name's Thomas. What the hell are you doing in a place like this, kid? Aren't you a bit high class for such an establishment?" he says, first addressing me, then this boy.

"What'chu two sayin o'r there?" Larry has finally paused to take a breath and several swigs of his second pint, now almost empty. Ivan just shakes his head at him, after which he grunts and continues to eat.

Ivan excuses himself. I stand up and allow him to exit the circular booth, but I don't bother to sit back down. I refuse to be at the table alone with the pig, so I leave him to his meal and make my way to the restroom.

For such a classy bar, the bathroom's a bit of a shithole. That's what I would think if the bar were *actually* classy. However, it is not. There are no stalls, no paper towel dispensers, no toilet paper, no soap. It's just a toilet in the corner of the room with a sink beside it, both of which are covered in spots of what looks to be mold. The room is finished with tiling on both the floor and walls, stained by what I can only assume to be an accumulation of bodily fluids.

I stand in awe for several minutes, not wanting to enter any further, but too disgusted to turn immediately away. The place I came to escape the reality outside has turned out to be worse. This thought brings me comfort, though. If a simple bathroom, albeit a terribly vile one, can be worse than the events of my life, then I can't be doing all that bad, can I? I turn around to return to the bar.

Ivan is standing at the bar, while Thomas, often glancing over nervously towards him, is wobbling on a bar stool, feet swinging, talking to the big, tattooed man. Thomas looks like a child. The conversation must be going reasonably well, though, because the bouncer-looking character, who I figure is interviewing Thomas, has a soft expression on his face, almost a smile.

Ivan and I make eye contact again, and he looks concerned and confused.

To make matters even more confusing, in through the door walks the last person I would expect to see in a place like this. Jill looks around, smiling innocently, ready to take on whatever comes her way. Her eyes fall on me and she grins widely. I don't even care about anything else happening around me. I don't even remember the disgusting bathroom or Larry the cop or my awkward position with Ivan. It's all gone.

* * *

*Laura*

Max has a more resilient spirit than anybody else in the world, Laura is certain of that. He sits on her lap the whole drive, not moving a muscle. When she parks, he looks up at her curiously before ambling over to the passenger seat, allowing her to get out.

"Do you want to stay in here, buddy?" she asks.

Max contemplates a moment before following her out of the car. He still limps, but doesn't let out a single cry on their walk into the station. The chief meets her at the door, puzzled, looking back and forth between Laura and Max.

"And who is this, Laura?" she asks.

"Sorry, chief. This is my dog, Max. Someone took him out of my yard earlier today. Long story short, he turned up at the shelter with quite the gash on his leg. I didn't want to leave him alone at home, so here he is."

Max sniffs the crisp crease of the chief's pants cautiously, head bowed. When he seems satisfied with the scent, the chief bends down and ruffles his ears tenderly.

"Hi, buddy," she says to him when he raises his eyes to meet hers.

"Sorry again for this, chief," Laura says.

"Don't worry about it. He's a good boy, isn't he?" She spoke more to Max than to Laura. "We've got some paperwork for you to look at, and probably fix too. Larry's doing, of course. I don't know why I keep him around, honestly. Max can sit with you inside; I'll find some cushions to make him a bed."

Max's tail swishes back and forth against Laura's legs, standing protectively between them. He grins up at them. The three walk inside together, where the chief finds some soft couch cushions to lay down by Laura's desk. Laura did have to put a fair effort into fixing Larry's paperwork. Not only was it formatted incorrectly, there were spelling mistakes and smudged ink that she had to decipher.

* * *

*Jill*

Call it intuition; call it luck; call it being pretty damn smart and using the Find My Phone app; call it whatever you want, but here she is, in this horrid dive of a bar, staring at that handsome (in a gentle, caring kind of way) bastard who has managed to make her quite affectionate toward him. It could be considered a bit strange, maybe even a bit psychotic—her using technology to track him down—but Jill calls it knowing what she wants and not being afraid to go for it. She calls it taking the necessary initiative.

Something changed in her after she met him, and although she's not giving him all the credit, he does deserve a little bit. She used to feel scared all the time, but there's a lot less to be afraid of now. She's growing into feeling really, truly great with herself—not because of his doing, but because of her own.

When she catches his eye, it's obvious that the feeling is mutual. She sees in his face that, at that moment, Jill is the only person in the room to him. Isn't that what everybody wants?

But something changes quickly. His face drops, and his focus shifts all around the room. She knows that she's made a mistake in coming here.

\* \* \*

It's a strange string of events, going from horrendously indifferent, to ecstatic, to concerned. My heart feels ready to just stop beating and let me die in that instant, and I consider pushing it to do so. It would be easier, at least, but I'm not taking the easy way out any more.

Jill approaches me with her face changing from glad to painted with worry— worry for me? Or perhaps that's just my own narcissism speaking, telling me I'm the only thing that could cause her concern.

What in the hell is she going to think of my being in a place like this?

What in the hell is *she* doing in a place like this? A casual after work drink at the scuzziest place in town?

I don't know, but I don't have time to weigh out options, as we hug tightly, without words, and then pull apart to examine each other's faces.

"Wha . . ." we both begin.

"What are you doing *here*?" I ask.

"I think I should be asking you the same thing," she says.

I can't argue with that.

"I came to find you," she tells me. "I know that sounds a bit creepy, but I swear I can explain and make it sound much more reasonable."

I hold up a hand. It feels unnatural and rude, but I allow it to happen.

"I mean absolutely no offense by this, but there is just too much going on right now. I'm just going to take you at your word and trust that you're not a complete lunatic. I think you've given me the benefit of the doubt, so I'd like to do the same," I say, the words not feeling like my own.

She raises her own hand, parallel to mine, and slaps hers against mine—a high five. She smiles knowingly and nods once. She leans her head against my shoulder. I wrap my arm around hers and give a gentle squeeze.

Thomas and the beefcake barman have finished their discussion. He's quit looking over at Ivan nervously, and as he is led behind the bar and shown where things are hidden, he actually appears quite in his element. Looking past them, I can see that Larry has completed his feeding time and is now looking around with a different kind of hunger, presumably for Ivan and myself, and tapping his empty pint glass aggressively against the table.

Now that I'm taking in my surroundings, it becomes obvious that we are the only customers here, and the tattooed man, the girl, and Thomas are the only employees. Thomas and his boss are both talking quietly and staring blatantly at Larry, although he doesn't notice in the slightest.

Ivan has come to stand with Jill and me. He taps my shoulder and points out what I've already seen. He seems nervous about whatever is about to transpire. Thomas looks back at us, and after exchanging one final look and few more words with his new boss, he approaches us. He doesn't even look at me at first, until Ivan and he exchange hellos.

"Hey, so this is a little weird, right?" Thomas asks him.

Ivan laughs. "You've got that right, kid."

"Listen, your friend over there, the big guy…"

"Don't call him my friend, please," Ivan says. "He's a co-worker. An acquaintance, at best."

"So, why are you here with him then?" Thomas asks.

"That's a terrific question," Ivan begins, shifting his attention to me. "Shall we get out of here?"

Then Thomas acknowledges me, realizing my presence, it seems, for the first time.

"Hi! Sorry. I'm Thomas, nice to meet you," he says quickly. Then, "No, you guys should stay, but I have to ask the big guy to pay his bill and leave. That was pretty much the only stipulation to me being hired. I guess Jimmy has seen what can happen after his third or fourth pint, and it's usually not pleasant. "

"Stipulation?" Ivan looks confused. "When did you become the type to throw around ten-dollar words?"

"There's a lot about me you don't know, I guess," Thomas says, shrugging.

"Likewise," Ivan says under his breath. "I can just tell him he needs to go, if you want."

"Would you be willing to do that? I just have to make it look like I'm the one kicking him out," Thomas says, quiet and coy.

"It's just favor after favor with you, isn't it, kid?" Ivan says mockingly.

"I'll discount your tab. How does that sound?"

"Can you even do that yet?" Ivan asks. "You've been employed for all of five minutes."

"Let me just ask my boss," Thomas says, and turns away. Before he even takes a step, Ivan has grabbed him by the collar and held him back. The boss man, Jimmy, has his back turned for this, luckily, or I'm sure we would all be physically removed.

"Don't do that, you dumbass," Ivan says.

Ivan looks at me and nods in Larry's direction, who now happens to be staring at us suspiciously, about to attempt standing up. Even from across the bar, I can see grease and sweat all over his face. I turn back to Jill, while Ivan and Thomas move towards Larry. It's obvious that Jill hasn't got much of an idea what's going on. Hell, I don't know if I do.

"It's kind of a long story," I say, "but I promise I will explain everything soon."

"I don't know if I actually want to know," she says.

I don't blame her. I feel horrible that she made the gesture of showing up here only to be faced with whatever this is, but I have no control over it. I suppose that's just something I should accept.

Our attention is drawn back towards the table I had previously been seated at, where a scene is now unfolding. Larry has failed to stand up so far, struggling to get his legs to balance his weight. It's hard to say whether the pints he sucked back like an animal lost in the desert are playing a part, but I have to think that they are, if only to avoid developing a sense of pity for the man.

"Ya'll think y'can just kick me out f'r no reason at all?" he mumbles.

"Look, we have several reasons to ask you to leave. Don't make me call the police," Thomas says, so quietly I can barely hear him from where Jill and I are standing. I begin to move closer. I don't want to be involved, but for some reason, I feel the absolute need to know what happens.

"I AM the damned PO-lice, ya little shit." Larry is losing it now, throwing his arms around in a temper tantrum.

Ivan steps forward, taking a stand between Larry and Thomas, who again has taken on the appearance of a little boy in comparison to the other two.

"Larry, if you don't walk out of here this second, you'll be spending the night in a cell, and I will personally request for your badge and gun to be confiscated," Ivan says calmly. "And you know the chief wants you gone; she's just waiting for a reason."

Larry pulls an arm back, hand pulled tight into a big, fat fist, but Ivan holds his ground and doesn't make a move other than drawing his right hand up and under his leather jacket to grip something I can only assume to be a gun. Larry relaxes slightly, looking wildly back and forth between Thomas and Ivan, grease still thick around his face. I half expect him to start foaming at the mouth and ripping into whatever bits of flesh he can get his teeth around.

He doesn't. In fact, he drops his arm to his side in defeat, and his face squishes up and appears ready to let loose a cascade of tears.

"Aright, boys. M'apologies," Larry says, pulling his wallet out and dropping a fifty on the table. "I'll just be goin' now. Evenin'."

I'm baffled by how unpredictable he's showing himself to be. I'm more frightened of him now than I was before. He begins to walk away, stopping only to look Jill up and down slowly. I step in front of her and stare into his eyes. I'm not normally the type to play alpha male, but I couldn't control my actions when that disgusting look took over his face. I step towards him as threateningly as I can manage, but he's already walking away again.

Jill rests a hand gently on my shoulder and tells me to relax without using her words. I know she can take care of herself, but I still want to be the one to care for her—not because she can't, but because I care. I suppose there's a part of me that needs to be needed so badly, because I haven't been in ages.

"I think I should go," she tells me.

I want to say no, but I think she should too. I just look at her blankly, trying to convey an apology that shouldn't be said with empty words, but with actions.

"I'm sorry," I say anyway, trying to make it clear that I mean it.

Ivan steps up to us and says his apologies as well.

"It's been a weird day," he says.

Jill and I nod in unison. No words. Just the strange, eerie silence that can only be heard, or felt, in an empty bar.

I hug her. I kiss her. I tell her to have a good night and that we'll talk about all this tomorrow, and it'll make more sense then, and she says okay and walks away.

I take my seat again at the table, and Ivan brings us both another drink. I don't even have to lean in to smell that it's whisky. I want to ask for ice, but more than that, I want to maintain a good image in Ivan's eyes, so I just sip it quietly and flex my entire body to make sure I don't visibly shudder. We sit in silence for what feels like a long time. Sipping our drinks. Making brief eye contact. Tapping our feet on the dirty floor.

"Well," Ivan says, breaking the silence. "I guess I owe you a bit of an explanation."

"I'd appreciate that very much," I tell him.

"So, Thomas and I met when I was black out drunk. I found him on my couch in the morning. Almost shot the kid, actually."

"Wow. Okay, and what about this Larry character? He's a cop? How does that work?"

"Yes, we do work together, although he doesn't do much real work. He's more the let-everybody-else-do-it kind of person."

"That's good. Makes me feel safe as a Prair Pass citizen." I make sure the words are dripping with sarcasm.

"Look, I'm not fond of it either, okay? I despise the guy more than you ever could, and I have to see him every single day—when he actually shows up to work, at least."

"Is tonight pretty typical behavior for him?"

"I couldn't tell you for sure. I make a point of not hanging around him outside of work. Hell, I mostly avoid him at work too."

"Well that's comforting," I say, finishing my drink bitterly and letting out a small twitch.

We return to silence, him sipping and me staring at the table. I still have questions, but I don't want to talk anymore. I'm becoming angry about everything and everybody, and I just want to go home and lock the door for a few days. I don't want to see anyone's face, speak to anyone, or explain myself to anyone. I've gotten good at pushing people away over the years. It's a bit of a habit, a defense mechanism maybe, and it works. Life's just easier for me when I'm alone.

I don't want to be here anymore. I want to sink into blank space and feel nothing and worry about nothing and have nothing. That sounds like suicide, I guess, but that's not what I want. I suppose I just want to be alone for a while.

I tell Ivan that I have to go, that I should call a cab and head home, and he looks like he wants to stop me from leaving, but doesn't say anything. I ask Thomas for my bill, and ask, without much hope, if he has a portable debit machine he can bring over to me, as I want to stay away from the big, scary man tending the bar. Of course they don't have one, so I have to approach the bar and make my payment there. He looks displeased with me still, even though he didn't have to deal with Larry.

I step outside and pull out my phone to call a taxi. As if in response to my thought, a cab pulls into the parking lot dangerously quickly and comes to a stop directly in front of me. Had I already made the call and somehow forgotten? There was nobody else inside who could have called. The driver looks at me, then down at something in his lap, and back up at me.

"Hey, your name don't happen to be Jill, do it?" he asks through his open window, tilting back his baseball cap to let the light shine on his face. It's an act that should make him appear more trustworthy, but it doesn't do much in that sense.

"No," I say. "She left a while ago. Another cab must have come already. Sorry."

He shakes his head, beginning to worry me.

"Nah, I'm the only driver on tonight. It's been dead slow all day. Did you see her leave? Maybe she decided to drive?"

That's strange. Maybe a friend came to get her, although based on her response to that idea last time I brought it up, it's doubtful.

"She doesn't drive," I tell him.

He shrugs his shoulders.

"Well if she ain't here, I'm not gonna be stickin' around. I could be back at dispatch snoozin'." He rolls up his window and tips his hat to me before driving away.

I try to think of the most reasonable explanation, but I can't find one. She could have decided to walk, but her house is at least a forty-minute walk, through parts of town that are less than desirable, and it's not all that warm an evening.

Realistically, though, what could have happened to her in a quiet parking lot in the ten minutes that she was out here alone? I recall my recent escapades in parking lots, and any comfort I was hoping to hold onto drains away quickly. I go back inside, where Thomas and Ivan are chatting as he pays his tab, and they both look up at me at the same time. Ivan rushes towards me; obviously, my face isn't concealing any of my worry.

"What is it?" he asks, seriously and soothingly.

"She's missing. Called a cab. It just got here, but she is nowhere to be seen."

I don't have to say anything more. Ivan is out the door, clearly in a rush and taking this seriously, but not trying to exacerbate my panic. Thomas just looks back and forth between me and the door, confused. I follow Ivan outside, where he's already pacing the length of the parking lot, looking down the street and doing something on his cellphone simultaneously. In the heat of the moment, I completely forgot that I could just call her and figure this all out so much more easily.

I reach into my pocket, pull out my phone, and call. I put the phone up to my ear, anxiously waiting for a ring. I hear one, both from the earpiece of my phone and from a glowing mess of mechanical parts on the ground a few feet away from me. I let my arm go limp and drop my phone to the ground, staring at the remains of my last hope of finding Jill easily.

Ivan's reached me by now and deduced what I just figured out.

"Shit," he says under his breath. "It could still be nothing, though. An accident, perhaps. Or maybe she was just pissed off." It's more for my sake than because he believes it, I think.

"What can we do?" I ask.

Ivan runs through a list of options, but he's gone into cop mode; he's not talking to me like a person, he's speaking to me like a victim, or a friend of the victim. I can't bring myself to listen, even if some of the options are reasonable.

"Look, you can't start to panic yet, all right? I'm sure she'll be just fine and turn up without a scratch," Ivan says.

"Can you put the word out to the rest of the cops in town? I know it's early, but please?"

He nods and takes a few steps away and makes the call, quietly.

"If anyone sees her, I'll be the first to know, and you'll be second," he assures me.

"That's all good and fine, but I still want to get out looking for her. Can you take me home to my car? I think we'll be more useful if we split up," I tell him, taking control of the situation as best I can.

"Yeah. Yeah, you're right. I want to go by Larry's first…"

"Why?" I cut Ivan off. "What good could that do us?"

"Look, nobody here is his biggest fan, myself included. But he was here, and he could have seen something that can help us."

"Fine," I say, "but we've got to make it quick. I don't want a second wasted."

Ivan nods and we begin walking to his car.

\* \* \*

*Laura*

Max falls asleep within minutes. He's never been a graceful sleeper. Snores rattle his entire upper half, his jowls quiver and lift to reveal pearly, white teeth.

Larry's paperwork needs to be entirely rewritten. Laura doesn't mind, though. She finds comfort in keeping herself occupied, and Max seems to be comfortable on his makeshift bed.

The ink-splotched, chicken-scratched twin of Laura's notes is a wrinkled mess of a pile in the corner of her desk. She dots her final *I* and crosses her last *T* before sweeping Larry's mess into the shredder. Max's ears perk up at the shredding sound, but only for a second, before his deep sleep continues. Laura removes a manila folder from a stack in her bottom drawer and places her paperwork neatly inside of it.

Laura considers waking Max up to walk with her to the chief's office, but sees his big, stupid grin snoring away and decides against it. She puts her computer to sleep, tucks the Manila folder under her arm, and walks past the mostly empty desks. A few stragglers glance up at her, tapping lifelessly away at their keyboards.

When she raps her knuckles gently against the chief's solid oak door and begins to push it open, Laura hears the chief muttering concernedly. By the time she's opened the door completely, the chief is returning her phone to her desk. Her face is set in a grimace.

"Shit. Shit, shit, *shit*," she says quietly.

"Sorry to interrupt. Is something wrong? I've got the paperwork Larry started here," Laura says, sliding the folder across the desk.

"We've got a missing person. Ivan just called it in. He sounded pretty shook up. Not exactly something I would expect from a guy like him. We've got to let everyone know."

"Not many people left here, Chief. Might have to call them in."

"I'll do that. I'm glad you're here, Laura. You're excused."

She picks up her phone again as Laura closes the door behind her. When Laura gets back to her desk, Max lies exactly where she left him, snoring happily.

\* \* \*

*Jill*

It's pitch black and Jill can barely move. She's not restrained—there simply is not enough room. Her first guess is that she has been buried, and that this is her coffin. Perhaps she's dead; if not, she's surely dying. The sound of squeaking brakes is what brings her back.

She's not dead, and she doesn't plan to die any time soon.

This isn't a coffin, this is a trunk.

Jill does the natural thing for someone trapped in the trunk of a car. She screams, and she kicks fiercely upwards. The sounds of her feet pummeling the interior of the trunk echo all around and make her head spin and her stomach threaten to purge all over herself and this small space. Fantastic, a concussion to top this all off nicely; that could explain her relative calm. This is no spa treatment, but she should be much more panicked than she is right now. That could work to her advantage. Jill gives her temples a gentle rub and attempts to look around, hoping to see anything at all.

Down around her feet, there seems to be a source of light, so she begins aiming kicks in that direction. On the seventh or eighth attempt, her left foot connects with something sharp enough to slice right through the canvas of her sneaker and into her big toe. She feels the warm moisture of blood begin to drench her sock. She lets out a cry of pain, but only for a second, before muffling it with her hand.

Jill's work wasn't for nothing, though; the light by her feet has grown vastly brighter, and she feels sure that she's managed to kick out a taillight, or at least loosen it. This means that, while she's relishing her small success, she can now see the full extent of the injury on her toe. Her shoe has gone from a light grey to a deep, blood red. It would actually be quite the nice color, if not for its source.

The thought sends her head spinning and her stomach churning once again, and she has to focus extremely hard to prevent passing out, or vomiting, or both.

She pulls herself together in time for the trunk to open, a bright light to blind her, and for everything to go black after feeling a shooting, burning pain in her neck.

\* \* \*

He definitely didn't go home, but where he did go remains a mystery. Ivan's taken us past Larry's house, a rundown mess of a building south of the highway, but there's no sign of him. Even Ivan seems to be growing seeds of doubt about his innocence. I swear, if he's laid a hand on Jill, I will bring the fucking hammer of street justice down on his ass. I don't give half a damn if he's police. Every muscle in my body was vibrating with adrenaline when I first sat in Ivan's car. The anger flowing through me made me want to act irrationally at first, to kick and punch inanimate objects and scream at the sky until she appeared, smiling, in front of me. Now, as we're pulling up to the curb in front of my house, my body has become still. All the rage has made me calm. It's made me sharp and focused. I'm ready to search and rescue. And revenge.

"Meet me at the station," Ivan tells me as I'm stepping out of his car.

"I want to look for her on my own. I can't sit around any longer," I say, about to slam the door.

"What are you going to do? Drive around in circles? You can't lose your mind over this. We'll find her. We just have to put our heads together."

"Fine." I nod, shutting the passenger door.

As I'm unzipping my pocket and pulling out my keys, I consider going inside to change. It hadn't dawned on me until now that I'm still wearing my running clothes. There's so many more important things to focus on, though, so I forget it completely and go straight to my car. Ivan has pulled away from the curb, but he's waiting in the middle of the road, watching me as if he's ready for me to do something stupid. I get in my car, start the engine, and I follow him just as he asked.

\* \* \*

We're at the station, asking the few cops on duty if anybody has seen anything or heard from Larry. Well, I suppose Ivan is doing most of the asking. I'm sitting by the entrance, thinking that maybe I should just walk out, continue to drive and hope that I'll stumble upon something, anything that could be helpful. I feel like I've wasted hours, days even, and Jill's still somewhere out there. I've gone over what I'm going to do when I find her at least a thousand times.

More specifically, I've gone over what I'll do to whoever's taken her, and every time it gets more gruesome. Broken limbs and bleeding orifices and fingers torn off and other body parts snipped with hedge clippers. I've thought of it all, and I don't even feel bad about it. Maybe this is going to be what pushes me over the edge, takes away my sanity, changes me for the worst. Ivan's told me over and over again that it could be nothing, but I know that's not true.

He returns to me with a blank disappointment obvious all over him.

"No luck?" I ask, getting to my feet.

"Nothing. Nobody's reported anything suspicious. Nobody can get a hold of Larry."

"What do we do in the time being then?" I ask. "I'm not just going to stand around. We don't have any time to waste. Why don't we head out and start looking, if they hear anything they can let you know." My voice rises steadily, almost reaching a shout by the time I'm done speaking.

I've grabbed the attention of everybody in the building. They all stare at me until I turn my gaze in their direction, and then they go back to typing away at their computers, or at least pretending to. Is it possible that they're frightened of me? Maybe they think I'm just another lunatic, ready to explode. Hell, maybe I am. I barely even know.

"Just take a seat for one second, okay?" Ivan urges me, trying to be the voice of reason. "If we go off on some wild goose chase, we'll still be wasting time. We need a plan. We need to discuss how we're going to deal with it if it's . . . bad."

Shit. He's trying to give me the 'She might be dead and buried, or even worse, and you need to be prepared for that' talk. That can't be a good sign.

"If that's the case, I think you know very well what I'm going to do," I say calmly.

"And I think you know very well that I will not be able to allow you to do that," he responds. "Look, I'm on your side, but I'm still a cop, and I still need to act like one."

"Are you on my side?" I'm raising my voice again, and have to make a physical effort to keep it hushed. "If you're on my side, Ivan, you'll let the real justice unfold. Don't try to stop me."

I get up and walk out of the station. If I stay any longer, I'll end up making an enemy out of the only friend I have left. I know he's on my side. He's just trying to do his job. But my rage is trying hard to take control, and it's tempting to allow it.

I sit down on the curb, let my head fall into my hands, and openly fucking weep. Cars drive by, slowing down to stare. Maybe they think to stop and offer help, but nobody does. The door opens violently, slamming into the wall and groaning shut. Ivan storms down the steps.

"You can be upset with the situation. You can be upset with me. But you cannot jeopardize my job. I want to work together. I want to help you. But I can't do that unless you get a hold on yourself."

He's not wrong, but I'm still so angry.

I'm about to muster a response when a cab pulls into the parking lot. The same driver from earlier looks at me with recognition before having a brief exchange with his passenger. Out of the car comes Thomas, the kid Ivan knows somehow, from the bar. He's pale and breathing heavily, looking back and forth between Ivan and me.

"I've got something you guys need to see," he says, holding up a USB stick.

"What is it?" I ask him before Ivan can speak.

"I… you'd better just watch it."

We go inside together. I'm shaking again, adrenaline flowing heavily at the prospect of this kid having something that could help. Most of the other cops carry on with what they're doing as if we're not even there. Only a tall blonde woman perks up in her chair and eyes us curiously. We pass a desk littered with balled up paper and

cheeseburger wrappers, the monitor covered in greasy fingerprints, where I'm certain Larry usually sits. Making our way to Ivan's desk clump, in the very back of the station, Thomas hands what I hope to be useful evidence over to Ivan. When he struggles, but finally succeeds in fitting the USB stick in to his computer, he turns to me before doing anything further.

"Maybe you shouldn't…" he begins, before I stop him.

"You know I have to, Ivan. You know that." I stare at him as sternly as I can manage at the moment. I'm so full of emotion that I can't even feel any of it any more.

I don't know why I insist, but I know that I have to. I have to see it. I need all of the anger, all of the hatred, to fuel me and keep me set on what I know I must do.

Ivan hesitates. He wants to fight me on this, but he's learning to pick his battles, it seems. He turns on his computer and brings up a video. He plays it.

I watch, unblinking, every last second of the video, then demand he play it again, and again, until I feel I'm about to vomit.

I see Jill, walking outside and looking rather flustered, making a phone call and then standing around waiting innocently. I see Larry, huffing and puffing, walk outside and stare at her for a long while before walking away and disappearing from the screen. I see Jill continue to wait, to stare down at her boots and appear deep in thought. I see the pig reappear with something in his hand, and quicker than he should have been able to, he touched whatever he held to her neck. Jill's body went limp in to his arms and Larry carried her away. He had no hesitation, no thought about what he was doing, as if it was natural for him.

Thomas realized that we needed to see this. When I look first at Ivan, then at him, they both have an apologetic look on their face, as if it's somehow their fault this is the way things panned out.

"We'll find him," is all Ivan says at first. "Don't worry. I swear, we'll find him."

"I didn't know if I should bring this to you or not. My boss told me not to get involved. But I figured, you know, this is pretty important."

"You did the right thing, kid," Ivan tells him.

My vision blurs, my pulse echoes through my head, and I think for a second that I'll pass out. I curl my hands in to fists and flex them until it hurts, bringing myself back to focus. My legs push me up to stand as if on their own accord, and I begin pacing back and forth taking shallow gulps of air.

"You're freaking out. For good reason, but I still need you to take some deep breaths and try to calm down. We're gonna give you a minute. I'm going to go let the chief know the situation, and we'll have people out there finding her immediately. Okay?" He tries to meet my eyes, but I can't manage eye contact right now, so he looks to Thomas and says, "Come on, kid. Give him a moment."

They leave me alone, and I continue pacing back and forth, digging my fingernails in to my palms.

\* \* \*

*Jill*

It's dark. Still. Jill's breath vibrates against cloth draped over her head, and as the spinning of her brain begins to slow, she can see what appears to be natural light filtering through it. Coming from some distant window or door, perhaps. There's a damp, underground sort of stench filling her nose, masked only by the bodily odor coming from what's covering her face. She's sitting upright on a hard, uncomfortable chair, and her back and ass are aching. Her ankles and wrists are taped tight to the arms and legs of her seat. The pain in her toe makes itself obvious once again, but it's alright. Her body maybe realizes that there are more important things to be worrying about, like how she's going to get out of here.

Someone's coming now, although she doesn't know where from. **139**
Jill hears deep, labored breathing. It seems in her best interest to
pretend she's still asleep, so she closes her eyes and begins to breathe
slowly, deeply, allowing what she hopes to be a natural twitch in her
pained foot every ten or twenty seconds.

Hot breath on her shoulder forms beads of perspiration that run
down her back and push a shiver through her body, but she fights
her bodily impulse and remains fairly still. Footsteps circle around
her, and the presence stands now directly in front of her. Fear is
beginning to take hold. She wants to scream and cry out for help,
to shake every muscle in her body in some attempt to free herself.
Keeping still and breathing steady is the hardest thing she can ever
remember doing. The cloth is ripped quickly off her head, only just
after she's squished her eyes shut, still hoping to maintain the façade
of sleep.

A warm, wet tongue runs up her cheek and breaks her completely.
Jill opens her eyes and screams directly into his face, which pushes
him back momentarily before a smile spreads over his sweaty face.

"Mornin', beautiful," he says.

Jill's eyes adjust slowly, vision blurring, then focusing, and finally
falling on a face she recognized, if barely. The large, sweaty police
officer she'd last seen being kicked out of the bar. She recalled the
way he'd looked at her so slowly, eyes moving up and down her body
as if appraising livestock. His beady little eyes are glowing with pleasure as he stares in to hers.

"Get the fuck away from me," Jill says.

"Na, don't go sayin' that, darlin'. I was hopin' we'd be good pals."
His breath smells like death, a mouthful of teeth un-brushed for
years. His face lifts into a jolly grin, then falls immediately to a con-
centrated frown.

He closes his eyes and breathes in deeply, close enough to her neck
to make her shudder and pull away as far as she can. Jill struggles
against the tape and the sturdy wooden chair; her hands are cold and

losing feeling. The only movements she can manage are to turn her head and lift her butt barely an inch off the seat. She strains again, realizing there's no possibility of getting loose.

Now that her face is uncovered and her eyes adjusted, she sees that she's in the centre of a small concrete room with no windows and only one door, through which the light had been creeping through. Besides herself, her chair, and her captor, the only other thing in the room is a tall metal table covered with brutish looking instruments: several knives, bits of copper pipe, thick wire clippers, and a long thin rod of shiny metal that comes to a sharp point. Through the open doorway in front of her she can see the middle of a staircase leading up to the right, the damp smell making sense as she realizes she's in a concrete basement. Under the staircase is a long plywood box, long enough to fit a human body comfortably, as long as that body did not plan on moving.

As she's seeing all of these things, her captor is walking away from her. She can hear the creak of old stairs as he ascends, threatening to give way under his weight. The throbbing of her toe has grown to the point of sending a pulse up her leg, through her spine, and into her skull. He must have stopped the bleeding somehow, or perhaps she's simply lost feeling, because she feels no more moisture. When Jill is certain he's reached the top of the stairs, after the sound of something heavy sliding across the floor and making a horrid grating sound, the impulse to freak out is finally let loose. She throws her shoulders back and forth against the chair, shaking her head errati-cally, trying to kick her legs but not managing to move them at all. She opens her mouth and out of it rips a blood-curdling scream she never thought herself capable of.

There's pacing back and forth above her, and something smashes against the floor and echoes down the stairs. Is this his home? Can somebody actually live in a place like this? It seems suitable only for rodents and pigs. Both of which, she supposes, could apply to the beast who has her taped up.

The pacing continues, back towards the stairs, and he begins to make his way back down slowly. What she can see of the staircase visibly bows under his weight, his face red with concentration, gulping a breath on every step. He enters the room, grinning at her, thumbs tucked in to his belt.

Jill needs to get the hell out of here. She rolls her wrists around, not even caring that he's right there, and the tape rips small hairs out of her arm, a pain that doesn't even register compared to the others she's felt, and surely will continue to feel if she doesn't get away. He walks in tight circles around her, not taking his eyes off her as she struggles, but making no effort to stop her either. The tape loses its hold on the skin of her right wrist and loosens up slightly from the movements.

He stops circling, standing again in front of her. Jill stops moving, and he smiles at her. Edging closer, his face grows serious.

When he gets within a foot of her face, he freezes. Not a movement, a blink, nothing. After a handful of disturbing seconds, she begins trying to free her wrists again, never taking her eyes off him. He blinks, and Jill stops moving. He slams fat hands down around her arms. Sweat immediately forms on his upper lip.

"N'that jus wouldn't do, would it, darlin'? Can't let you leave the party too early now," he says.

He reaches behind his back, pulling a fresh roll of pink duct tape from an unknown pocket. He wraps fresh layers up and down Jill's wrists, sweat dripping from his forehead onto her legs.

"I e'en got a perdy color for ya, 'coz I'm just that sweet, you know," he says, not quite a whisper.

"Please," she begins, taking a different approach, "I won't tell anybody, I swear. I'll just walk out the door, and you'll never see me again."

It's not true, and he knows it. If she gets out the door, the first place she's going is the police station. Ivan would believe her, even if the rest of them refused to.

"Na, I can't let you be doin' that. You know it too, don't ya?" he says. "'Course you do. Yer a smart little cookie, you. I can tell by y'r eyes."

"Listen, you sick fuck. You do anything to me, and you'll be rotting in prison the rest of your life. You know that too, don't you?" She's got her strength back, whether from anger or adrenaline. She mocks him a little bit with her question, but she doesn't think he'll pick up on that.

He stops for a second, his face screwed up in an attempt at thought. The sweating intensifies.

"Well, you'w'd be right. That is, if ever they could find ya. Or any the rest of 'em, for that matter." He starts laughing, increasingly hard, until he has to pause to catch his breath.

Jill begins to cry. She can't accept that she's going to die in this shit hole with this sick bastard. She won't accept it, but she knows she'd better start to try.

The tears have blurred her vision, and she decides to close her eyes and let whatever happens happen. But Jill can feel cloth wiping away the moisture from her face, gently.

"No tears, darlin'. Not yet."

* * *

Sitting around here isn't accomplishing much of anything, and I can't help but think of what could be happening to Jill every minute that we're wasting here. If they find her their way, that's great, but if I find her quicker then that's much better. I'm certain I have to get going, but not before I look through Larry's desk. It becomes quite obvious that he's not the only one around here to shirk his duties, as nobody even gives me a glance while I skim through the drawers of his desk and find some things that probably should have been kept on his person at all times.

Just as I am about to reach down into collect these items, a vaguely familiar grunting startles me to stillness. I lean back on my heels,

peeking around the corner of the desk. There, laying comfortably on top a pile of pillows, is the injured old pooch that I'd only recently left in the care of the animal shelter. His jowls rumble happily as he snores away.

A gun is sitting at the bottom of this drawer, looking much more like a toy and far less dangerous than I've always imagined one would. I don't know much about firearms, but it has six rounds and seems like it could probably kill a man. In the same drawer is a small notebook, and because I don't think he's the writing type, I grab it and hope it has something that will prove useful for me. As I'm pulling it out of the drawer, an office chair squeaks directly beside me.

"What do you think you're doing, sir?" the tall blonde woman asks me. She had been the only one showing any interest in what was going on earlier. Taking her in from the floor, I realize the full extent of her stature. She could easily drag me out of the station if she felt so inclined.

"Uh . . ." I fumble for words. "I'm just looking."

"You're going to have to be leaving now," she says, standing authoritatively over me. At the sound of her voice, Max perks up his ears and opens one eye. At the sight of me, he tries to stand too quickly and lets out a yip.

"Easy now, Max," she says to him, not taking her eyes off me.

His tail begins to wag, and he waddles over to me, slowly.

"Max, no. Lay down, boy," she says. But he ignores her, getting his big, goofy head under my hand and forcing pets out of me.

"Hey, old boy," I whisper.

"Sir, sorry about him. He wouldn't usually approach someone like that. You've got to leave, though." She notices the notebook in my hand and holds out an open palm. "Hand it over. That's police property."

I hand over the book, as Max's tail is sweeping the floor in front of me, looking back and forth between myself and his master. Something clicks in her expression. Not recognition, exactly, but something like it.

144 "Your leg's looking better, buddy," I tell Max.

"You're . . . you took him to the shelter, didn't you? He's never warmed up to anybody this quickly. He's friendly, but not *this* friendly." As if to confirm her words, Max licks my face gently and smiles up at her.

"Who did this to him?"

I rub Max's ears while I'm standing up, trying to appear as far from threatening as I can manage. "Some kid. He took my wallet too. Had your dog on a chain, so I followed him home. He got what he deserved. I got my wallet back. You got Max back. Everybody's happy, I'd say."

I offer an encouraging smile. She doesn't speak. She doesn't smile, either. But she looks down at her dog with anger painted over her body. After a while, she raises her eyes to me.

"This kid, he did this to Max?" She jerks her head back towards him, where he's returned to his spot atop the pillows.

I nod.

She drops the notebook on the floor.

"Oops. Now, you'd better get out of here." She sits back down in her chair.

I wait a moment before bending down to pick up the notebook. Max cracks his eyes open just a sliver when I'm down on his level. I give him a wink while tucking the book into my jacket and standing to walk away.

"He's a piece of work, you know," she says, without looking at me. "Larry, I mean. I hope you find what you're looking for."

I nod and exit the building quickly.

* * *

*Ivan*

Even after explaining the situation to the chief, and in turn, to the rest of the officers, they're all sitting on their asses staring at their computers.

Bullshit.

Ivan's the only one around here actually trying to do his job, and he gets shit all for it.

He cleans some things from his desk angrily, and then takes his gun and his badge, along with all the information gathered so far on Larry, which is neatly wrapped in a generic, manila folder.

As he's heading for the door, the nerdy little IT guy that had been assigned to look through Larry's hard drive came racing out of his little office in the back, shouting for Ivan to wait.

"Hey! Detective Ivan! Hold up," he says. "I found an address for you, for the cabin. Amongst a mess of other really disturbing stuff. This guy's kinda . . . super messed up, I'm telling you right now. It's a wonder we never found any of this before. Really messed up. He-should-already-be-locked up kind of messed up, if you know what I mean."

Ivan thinks he does. He takes the address and rushes to get out the door, hoping he can catch up before any rash decisions are made. But the IT guy stops him once more.

"Detective Ivan! Wait! One more thing, okay?

Ivan is growing quite impatient.

"Hurry up, kid. Spit it out. I've got shit to do," Ivan tells him. Poor guy. He's just trying to help.

"The guy you had with you. Your friend—the older one. When I was taking Larry's hard drive back to his desk, I saw him looking through his stuff. Figured I should come tell you or one of the other officers, because that's probably pretty illegal, right? So, I saw him searching, but Laura stopped him. So I figured it's okay, she'll handle it."

"Get to the point! Quickly, kid, quickly." He doesn't have time for this shit.

"He walked out with a notebook. I'm not sure how he got it past Laura, or even if it's any kind of big deal, but I saw him do it. I'm certain of it."

Ivan takes a glance over the occupied desks, looking for Laura, and when he can't find her, he's out the door in an all out sprint.

* * *

The sun is setting behind the mountains, casting a dark purple glow through the treetops, and it seems the perfect dramatic setting to kill a crooked cop.

I know what I need to do. When I reach Larry's house, I sit in my car and begin to skim through the pages that he's written. The little notebook told me the horrific details of the things he's already done and plans to do in the future. The exact number of people he's taken already remains unclear, but Jill is not the first.

*Their bodies are buried all round the cabin, waiting for the others to join 'em.* The last page says. I won't let Jill be one of the others. The idea that this information sat in his desk inside the police station makes me want to slap every Prair Pass Police officer across the face. How could they not have found him out? How could they let him get away with this?

I step out of my car and leave it unlocked, hoping that finding what I need won't take long. In the notebook, he spoke of *the cabin* constantly. I'm sure this is where he's taken Jill, and I must figure out where it is. His house represents him as a person quite well. The dirty, yellowed vinyl siding is peeling from under the windows in large strips. The front door is a frail bit of wood with a large piece of smoky glass at eye level. But I think better of trying to enter this way. I walk around the side of the house, through a gate so broken apart it's barely doing its job any more, in to the backyard. The yellow grass and weeds have grown up past knee height and over the concrete path, but I follow it anyway, leading to his backdoor, which is nothing more than a sheet of dirty glass with a handle. I try the handle first, knowing it won't budge, before removing my jacket, wrapping it around my arm, and slamming my elbow through the door. I expect resistance, but it shatters under the force quite easily. Reaching through the hole I've made, I jiggle the lock until I can open the handle and enter Larry's residence.

The exterior of the house was hard on the eyes. The inside is 147 worse, on all of my senses. There's an overall smell of rot, with oddly sweet and sour undertones. I need to search for an address, directions, or anything to lead me to his cabin, but I'm genuinely scared to touch anything. Through the back door, I've entered in to his kitchen, though it doesn't appear to have been used for cooking in some years. Styrofoam containers, growing black and green spots of mold, are stacked up in the sink. There are no plates or dishes in sight, though a corner of the room is dedicated to plastic pop bottles.

I cover my mouth with my shirt, not wanting to breathe in any of this acrid air, and begin to explore the rest of the house. Down a hallway, in his living room, I'm surprised to see stacks of books, though when I get closer, I realize they aren't novels, but notebooks. Dozens of them. I pick one off a leaning tower and flip to a page, where I find more gruesome details of kidnap and torture and finally murder and burial.

The scent already had my stomach on edge, but looking at all of the notebooks, and realizing the depth of what he's done, pushes my guts over the edge. I vomit in front of the books, in to the carpet that has become a tangled, stained creature living on the floor. But I know I need to keep looking. There's simply no time to feel sick and disgusted. I wipe the tears from my eyes and leave this room for another, his bedroom. A mattress is tucked in one corner of the room, a pile of stinking clothes in the opposite corner. Besides that, the room is empty, so I leave it behind, growing more frustrated and more angry. I pass the bathroom without a second thought, not feeling capable of entering any room Larry has shit in. Stepping back in to the living room, I notice something I'd missed before on the wall beside the front door. It's a large photograph of a dingy cabin in the woods, and beside it, a poorly drawn but detailed map. I have to step over my regurgitated bits of bile to reach it, and I knock over many books on the way, but when I'm able to see it clearly, I have no doubt where it leads. Prair Pass is labeled clearly, as is the highway going through it, and just off the highway up through the mountains is a smaller road leading to the cabin. All around it, red push pins have been stabbed through the paper in to the wall. I can only assume what they symbolize.

I leave the house in a hurry, knocking over more books and nearly tripping over a coffee table I'd barely been able to realize was there. Gulping fresh air when I finally get outside, I retrace my steps through the yard and get in to my car, driving off urgently.

* * *

### Ivan

The bastard managed to get gone much faster than Ivan could have imagined. He's driven, he has to give him that. Ivan knows where he's trying to go, but not if he knows how to get there. But he can't be worried about that. He just needs to get there himself. Jill's a sweet girl, as far as he knows. He doesn't want to think about what's been done to her, or he may end up being the one to murder Larry.

Ivan hasn't entirely figured out how he's going to perform an arrest. All he can do is hope that he'll be capable of overpowering Larry when it comes down to it. He's big, but Ivan can't see a lot of his girth being made of muscle.

The GPS tells him it will take twenty minutes to drive out to the cabin. Ivan's hoping to do it in ten.

* * *

### Jill

She's getting out. Jill has made the conscious decision. He watched her cry and wiped her tears for a while, but she refused to look at him, to see the look on his face as he did it. He must have grown bored of her when the tears stopped. He left her alone to return

upstairs. Since then, she's managed to wiggle her arm enough that her wrist can almost slip under if she squishes her hand together tightly. It hurts badly, but she only begins to notice when she stops working at it and allows her brain to feel it.

She has other things to think about. The deep, dark, animalistic part of her wants revenge in a horrible way. The thoughtful side knows she could never live with herself. But still, he shouldn't be allowed to get away with this, to potentially do it again.

She is getting ahead of herself, though. She hasn't even freed one wrist yet, and already she's thinking of what to do afterwards.

Focus, Jill, focus! She mouths the words as they go through her head.

Footsteps are descending the stairs, slowly and menacingly, but they stop after a few steps. Then, a new sound breaks the silence. It travels through the ground and permeates the cement room to echo all around her. It sounds like the crunching of dirt under a slow-moving vehicle. The steps retreat back upstairs.

Jill continues to wrestle with the tape, yanking aggressively now, unafraid to make a ruckus. Screams tear out of her throat without her control, but in return, she hears only the sound of a heavy door sliding and slamming shut upstairs.

The pink duct tape gives way just as the sounds of the car come to an abrupt halt after coming slowly closer and closer. Jill frees her right arm, takes the briefest second to embrace its freedom and move it around, and rips the tape from her other wrist before freeing her legs.

Jill has halted her screaming. Now is the time to be sneaky. She knows she needs the help of whoever has shown up outside, but she needs to get out of this basement first. Adrenaline pumps through her veins, her hands tremble and knees wobble. When she's about to step through the doorway, out of the dark, cement room, a series of noises upstairs holds her in place. Two voices shout over each other.

She hopes against hope that it's that cop, Ivan, who is verbally battling with Larry right now.

The decision to scream or not to scream seems like one that could at this point choose her fate.

She keeps her mouth shut and steps through the door. To her left is the bottom of the staircase, the rest of the basement is nothing but walls made of cement, and a small window far out of her reach. There's no other way out. A bulb sways at the top of the creaky old stairs, but it isn't lit. Jill finds herself quite surprised the stairs have managed to hold up under the weight of the house's owner.

There's no furniture down here, but in the space under the stairs, where the monster always hides to reach out and grab at your ankles, is the poorly constructed plywood box. No, perhaps not a box but a coffin, the lid of which is slightly askew, with a pile of nails and a rusty old hammer lying on top. She can only guess what that's for.

\* \* \*

"Where the fuck is she, Larry?" I spit, my rage filling my face with blood and putting a pulse through my eardrums.

I push him again, against the dusty old gas stove, always keeping the tip of the knife pointed at his face. He falls weakly, like a top-heavy toddler, not fighting me in the slightest.

"Please!" he screeches at me. "I'll tell yeh where she is, jus' don't hurt me!"

"You can't play the victim here, you sick bastard. I know what you've done. You know what you've done. Just tell me where she is, then I'll decide what happens to you." I can't stop screaming. My throat is raw, and I know it would be more productive just to speak to him calmly, but I can't calm down.

He begins to laugh, low at first, but escalating into a high-pitched cackle, staring at me the whole time and spitting all over his own face.

"I dun' think you'll wanna be seein' her, she ain't feelin' too hot, if yeh know what I mean." He winks, and for a second I'm sure he's killed her already. I take a step toward him, brandishing the knife intentionally, but the thought of Jill being dead is too much.

My knees buckle and I hit the floor hard.

"Where is she, Larry? Just tell me where. What did you do to her? What the fuck did you do?" Hysterical words come spilling out between gasps for air. The hand holding the knife becomes weak, just like the rest of me, and while it's dropping down to my side, he's standing over me grinning.

"Let me show you," he says, before smashing a ceramic mug over my skull and the light and my anger and everything else fades to black.

* * *

### Jill

The shouting upstairs has continued to escalate, and the violence seems to have evolved to something physical. Things crash to the floor, glass breaks, and the voices stop completely. Silence.

The heavy metal door at the top of the stairs begins to slide open. Jill hadn't calculated a reaction for this. She wasn't prepared. She goes to the only place she can think of, she steps quickly to the place under the stairs, slides the lid off the coffin, and lays down inside of it. It's a perfect fit. Compared to the last handful of hours of her life, she could almost call it comfortable. She slides the lid back over top of her coffin, eliminating the light, closes her eyes for a moment, and she listens.

There's steps on the stairs, as she expected, but something else follows them. A weight dragging across the floor, then thumping on to the first step. This is repeated down every stair—two steps down, then a dragging sound, and finally a thump. At every thump, Jill is certain the stairs will collapse right on top of her, but by some small miracle, they don't. The person stepping and the person being dragged reach the bottom.

She can't handle the idea of opening her eyes, of pulling back that coffin lid to see who was being dragged down the stairs and who was doing the dragging, but she can't hide for much longer.

They're near by the box now. By her estimate, they've come to the entrance to the room she was previously bound to a chair in. And they're still, and silent. A moment, two, three—several—pass by, and still there isn't a noise. Only then, a stir, and one solid *thud* of a fist on concrete.

"Sheeyit fuck, nah, oh shit nah, damn it!" Larry yells out angrily, echoing through the basement.

Jill hears him pound his fist against the wall three more times before he begins to laugh. The body she now knows not to be his slumps loudly to the floor.

"I'ma find you, little girly. I swear I am. Can't've gone too far, could ya?" he asks the open basement.

Jill is laying in the only hiding space there is down in the basement. He knows where she is. There's no way he doesn't.

He heaves loudly and lifts the body up again. Hopefully it's the body of a cop who has already called for back-up, who has his police friends screeching down the highway coming to help them both at that very moment.

"Come on now, fella. Let's get you all comfy, cozy n' situated a'right?"

The only opportunity Jill is going to get is presenting itself. While he's busy, she has to do something. Should she run up the stairs and out of wherever she's being held? Or does she try to help whoever is being tied to the very same chair she just managed to get out of?

She can't leave them behind. She wouldn't want to be left behind.

Slowly, she slides the lid to the coffin away, lifting it slightly, so the wood doesn't scratch against itself and grab Larry's attention. Although he's slow, she needs him not to notice her or the plan will

be foiled before she even figures out what it is. She can hear him grunting and groaning, and the sound of tape ripping off the roll. Shallow breaths from the other person break any silences.

She raises her head an inch, then another, until she can just see over the edge of her resting place. Larry's back is to her, so she rises slowly, like a vampire—dead before, but returning for blood. Jill steps out of the box and moves forward without a sound. She pauses when he pauses, breathes when he breathes, and only when she sees who is knocked out and taped to the chair does she inhale a quick gasp of air.

Did he hear?

He halts his movement abruptly, but continues after releasing a deep belch. She continues forward, so slowly it seems it will take an hour to reach them, but soon she's crossed the threshold into the room. Jill stares at the heavy eyelids, movement obvious beneath them, and the slight rise and fall of his chest. He's not dead. She wouldn't be able to live with herself. The table of metal instruments is pushed back against the wall beside her, things she doesn't want to imagine him using: pliers, knives with rough serrated edges, assorted shears and scissors. Jill selects the least brutal looking object on the table, a length of dense copper pipe. The weight feels good in her hands. It gives her a courage that she didn't know she needed.

She raises the blunt weapon over her head as she continues to step forward, but something goes awfully awry, something she hadn't thought of. His eyes open abruptly and fall not on Larry, but on Jill, and they go wide with fear and concern—and Larry notices. As he begins to turn towards her, quick for a man of his size, she puts her weight on her injured foot and, ignoring how much it hurts, kicks out with all of her strength. The bottom of her good foot connects hard with the side of his kneecap, and she feels a disgusting crunch beneath it.

He lets out a high-pitched cry and collapses to the ground, letting out one more yelp before he reaches towards his waistline for something, fumbling for it beneath his belly. Jill finds her balance quickly, raises the pipe over her head, and brings it down hard on Larry's forehead just as he is turning to face her, the gun in his hand almost coming to stare directly into her eyes before his body goes limp.

She steps over Larry's body, prodding him once with the pipe to make sure he's really out, and then feels her body begin to go into shock.

She manages to look into those desperate eyes, which were looking at her with more care than she'd seen before in her entire life. She pulls the tape gently from his mouth and runs a finger affectionately over his dry, cracked lips.

"Are you okay?" he croaks.

"Me?" Jill actually manages a laugh. "Look at yourself!"

He cracks the smallest of smiles, and she begins to unwrap the thick layers of tape, but when their eyes meet again, his are filled with a blind hatred. He's staring down at Larry as if he's forgotten she's there. The look on his face frightens her, enough so that she actually stops unwrapping the tape.

"We're going to get out of here, okay?" Jill says calmly, hoping to stifle his anger.

"Jill, I need to do something before we get out of here. You don't need to be a part of it, but I need to do it," he says.

Of course, she knows exactly what he wants to do. He wants to hurt Larry like Larry wanted to hurt her, like he probably would have hurt him. The look in his eyes is just the same as she'd seen in Larry. He wants revenge. She can't say that a part of her doesn't want the same. Jill wants to make him feel pain, and she wants to see the fear in his eyes that he so despicably tried to put in hers. But she knows that she has to keep that line between them.

Jill doesn't want to be that way. She doesn't want to be like Larry.

"Just think about this for a second, please. Please, please," she whispers, now cautious to avoid waking the beast at her feet.

"Oh, I have thought about it. I know exactly what I want to do to him, and how," he says, an evil in his voice that she doesn't want to hear.

"That's not who you are!" Jill shouts, throwing caution to the wind.

"Then who am I? Because I don't think I really know. And if I'm not the one to stop him, then who will be? The police? We've seen what they're capable of, and it's nothing all that great."

She says nothing. She just continues to unwrap tape until his left arm is free and he can do the rest for himself. Her back rests against the wall, and she looks at a man that she loved turned into someone she can't.

He's free. She shies away from him as he stands up.

"Please, can't we just go?" she asks once more.

"He's done this before. A number of times, to a number of people. I went to his house. I found notebooks filled with such gruesome, realistic details that I know they can't be made up."

"Even if he did, even if you're right, why does it need to be you who deals with it?"

He doesn't answer, only bends down to pick up the gun from where it's fallen beside Larry's body.

"He's a sick fuck. I know that better than you. But he should be in prison, not executed," Jill says.

"Maybe an execution is the only way to help. What did he do to you?" he asks, scolding.

Jill doesn't answer. She just wraps her hands around his arm and pulls him towards her, gently.

"You don't need to be this person," she says.

"No, you don't understand. I absolutely do need to be this person. This is the only purpose I've ever had, the only thing I've done that means anything," he says.

He raises the gun as the sound of an approaching car interrupts his thought process and slows his actions.

### *Ivan*

Ivan doesn't know exactly how, but he found the place. His car is parked outside Larry's cabin, in between two other cars on the dirt road. The building is rustic at best, a bit of a dump honestly, although Ivan supposes it's a suitable habitat for its owner.

The front door screen is ripped and it's near impossible to guess if that's recent or not. There are cracked windows and missing shingles all over the place, so it fits in quite nicely.

From outside, it appears that there are only two rooms. A small kitchen serves as the entryway, which leads to the right into a barely larger living room—neither of which appears to have anybody in them. Ivan begins to fear for the worst. He turns off his car, reassuring himself on the placement of his pistol under his leather jacket, and steps into the biting cold of the night. He tries to step quietly, but dense dirt with a thick coating of dry pine needles echoes crisp crunching sounds from underfoot, so he abandons stealth and runs quickly for the door.

A peek inside and the sound of total silence tells him nobody is in there, but the air itself seems to want to warn him about something. Ivan can only hope they haven't made their way into the woods, where it will be impossible for him to find them without being guided by the sound of gunfire, which he both hopes for and against all at once.

The door creaks loudly against the silence as he pulls it open just enough to sneak through. If there's anyone here, they're definitely aware of his presence now.

* * *

The gunshot was louder than I ever would have expected. It rippled through my entire body, sending vibrations from my fingertips to the ends of my toenails. My hearing was gone before I even saw the wound in Larry's skull start to seep blood and bits of brain. I guess that's what I get for firing a gun in a concrete basement.

Jill has fallen to the floor behind me. She's clutching her ears and crying, unable to look at me.

What have I done?

Is this justice, or some selfish form of revenge?

If it's revenge, then for what? If what I've done can be hurting Jill this much, then was it really the right thing to do?

She didn't read what I read about the others, though, the horrific things that Larry has done to them. The ones that spent just as long if not longer than her bound to that chair suffering whatever sick ideas came to his brain. But can I even be sure that is truth, or have I simply believed that because it's what I want to be true, because deep down, I really just wanted to kill him for what he could have done, regardless of what he did do.

Jill could be right.

Larry could have just been a sick, twisted man plagued with sick, twisted ideas.

My time to rationalize or punish myself for these actions has run out, as footsteps pound quickly down the stairs, and I can faintly hear a gruff voice yelling through the ringing that has only just begun to fade.

I suppose this means my time to face the penalties of my actions has come. There's nowhere to run. Even if there was, I still wouldn't be able to escape myself. An individual can make themselves suffer much more than anybody else can. I'm no exception.

My eyes fill with tired, self-loathing tears, and I let my gaze fall to where Jill rests on the floor. She's trembling. When I step towards her, to apologize, to try and do anything that would make her stay in my life, she pulls away. That's a good thing, maybe, probably, because I don't deserve her to stay.

**158**     I wipe my face with a dirty sleeve and look to the doorway, where a gun is pointed at me and Ivan is staring without a word.

\* \* \*

*Ivan*

Ivan breaches the corner to see one of the saddest sights he can remember. Jill is on the floor, retreating from everything around her. Larry's body is limp, and what's left of his head is leaking blood and brain matter all over the floor.

The gun is in the hands of the saddest person in the room. He's staring down at it as if it fired without his consent. The murder he's clearly committed was all he wanted, and now that he's done it, he would do anything in the world to undo it. But some things can't be taken back.

Ivan has his gun pointed at him, and finally the sad man takes notice of his presence. Tears are streaming down his face, and Ivan isn't sure what his reaction will be, or if he's even sure himself.

\* \* \*

*Jill*

She never would have thought him capable of something like this. Capable of murder. The worst part, as selfish as this may be, is that he did it—in part—for her. He did it to protect her. She begged him not to do it. Yet still, in some complex way, Jill puts some of the blame on herself. She accepts responsibility for something entirely out of her control.

The noise eliminated everything else in the world for a split second. The lack of sound and ability to feel was so peaceful that for a moment Jill thought he had turned the gun on her. She almost hoped. That just seems like it would be so much easier than this.

But she opens her eyes to find herself still there, and him still standing there, only something had changed so vastly in him in such a short blink of time. All of his pain and all of his regret, everything that he had ever felt, and all the mistakes he had ever made, are plain on his face. She sees what a broken man he truly is, that nothing was ever going to be okay for him again. And she doesn't know if she ever wants it to be, if she thinks he deserves to feel alright after what he's done.

She can see that he finally allowed himself to be weak and selfish, to act only on what he himself thought to be right, with no consideration for anyone else. And she can see how much it has already begun to tear him apart.

Jill's eyes fall back to rest on the floor, the only place she can look without turning away.

* * *

"Ivan, I have to go," I say between deep, strenuous breaths.

"I can't let you, and you know that," he says. "This is murder. You understand that, don't you?"

I tremble and drop the gun to the floor.

"I had to—"

"You didn't," Jill whispers from the floor, not raising her head. "He was already unconscious."

"You shot him while he was already knocked out? Who are you helping here? To think I was crazy enough to support you in the first place. God damn it, what the hell have I allowed you to do?" Ivan asks.

"You're right. Okay? You are. But I have to go. You know I have to go, and we both know you're going to let me," I say.

"How in the hell do you reach that conclusion? You're a fucking sociopath. You had me convinced you were doing a good thing here," Ivan says, hate burning up inside of him. Hatred for me.

I begin to walk towards him, and he raises his gun quickly.

"Don't think for a second I won't shoot you if you take one more step," he says. Then, shifting his attention and softening his voice, he calls, "Jill, hey, are you okay? What happened down here?"

She just shakes her head and buries her face in her hands.

"What did he do to her?" Ivan asks me, nodding towards the now nearly unrecognizable bits of brain and mess of blood on the floor above Larry's large body.

"I don't know," I say. "But look, there were others. I'm pretty sure."

"What?!" Ivan erupts. "Other people involved? Where did they go?"

"No, not that. Other people that Larry took before. I'm almost certain of it."

"What makes you think that?" Ivan asks.

"I found a book in his desk, and about forty more at his house. They were filled with gruesome detailed descriptions of the things he's done. You'll find all of them there. And there's a map, that's how I got here, it's covered in red push pins. I think it's where he's buried all the others."

"Oh, shit," Ivan says, beginning to lower his gun. "Look, even if you're right, I already called in back up. They may take a while to get here, but even if I wanted to, even if I decided to believe you, I couldn't let you go."

"Have I lied to you yet?"

He pauses, holstering his weapon and shifting his attention once again to Jill on the floor. He offers her a hand.

"Let's get out of this god forsaken room for now," he says gently.

Jill takes his hand and pulls herself to her feet, struggling briefly before he has her arm around his shoulder, bearing her weight. She tries to look into my eyes for any inkling of a good man, but I doubt she finds it. I doubt it's there.

We leave the room behind, slowly, and I take one last look back at what used to be a man named Larry. I know deep inside me that

I've done the right thing, and that the bodies of the other women he killed will be found somewhere nearby. He doesn't deserve the comfort of a prison cell.

\* \* \*

*Ivan*

God. Damn. I did not sign up for this kind of thing, he thinks. He assumes it's not uncommon for most kids becoming cops to expect all the action to be fun. But the shootouts never end in murder, just a non-fatal wound that the criminal recovers from in prison, where they pay for their crimes and become decent people somehow. Ivan didn't expect all that, but by no means was he prepared for this.

He doesn't really know what to think any more. This guy is clearly a little mad, but who is Ivan to say if it's the good kind of mad or the bad kind? Ivan's a fuckin' nobody, and he's totally fine with that, but now he's become wrapped up in something that he is not permitted to play the role of a nobody in. He's got to be a super detective, knowing every right from wrong, and who deserves what, and how to let the good guys keep being good, and lock up the guys that can do nothing but bad.

The shooter and the shot are just two varying degrees of evil, really, except one thinks they have justice on their side.

There are no good guys, not any more, Ivan thinks. We all play that part in our own minds, but shit, who can really say that they are a completely good person?

His mind is running away with him, his thoughts becoming more and more difficult to piece together.

"He didn't hurt me. Not really. I know he wanted to, and he would have, but he didn't get to because you intervened," Jill says. "So, for that, I guess I have to thank you."

She's not speaking to Ivan, barely aware he's even there; she's staring, coldly, at the other man, the one with blood on his hands. The thank you is hollow, full of resentment.

"But he was already knocked out," she continues. "You didn't have to pull the trigger. You know that. I know that. And Ivan knows that. The rest of the police will know it too."

Ivan knows he shouldn't let him go. He knows he can't. But for some reason, be it fate or another compelling force that he simply can't understand, he wants to. Never before has he believed in second chances.

So why now?

* * *

Ivan is beginning to break; I can feel it in the air around him, in the sound of his voice. He looks around at the trees and breathes slowly and deeply, inhaling the fresh air and trying to think clearly.

"They'll be here soon," he says. It sounds like a warning, rather than a threat. I've come to know the difference in his tone through the short time we've spent together.

They both stare at me, Ivan and Jill, and the guilt hurts deep. I want to run and hide away from it.

But the running has to stop soon. I've grown tired and sore, and my body simply won't accept much more. When it gets to a point that has to be forced, sometimes it's better just to let a thing quit.

"I'll be going now," I say, matter of factly.

Ivan just nods and walks away, leaving Jill to either stand on her own or shift her weight towards me. I'm grateful when she chooses the latter, even if it's only to avoid falling to her knees. If there's one last thing I can give her after all of this, I'm glad it can be to hold her up when it's too painful to stand on her own.

She shifts slightly to give me a knowing smile, not to express forgiveness, but to share a special kind of love that can only be had when you truly want to despise somebody. I smooth the hair on her head and leave words unspoken, holding her close and trying to express my love in more subtle ways—a gentle squeeze, an honest exhalation of pain, a silence.

I let her go.

The best things for those you care about and even for yourself can sometimes be the hardest.

I walk slowly to my car, wanting to stop, wanting somebody to stop me, but I don't and they don't and I keep on my path. Ivan throws me a set of keys I wasn't aware he had taken from me, one final gesture as a friend instead of a cop, and he turns away to stare down the road.

I get in my car, start the engine, and reverse slowly. I begin to drive back to Prair Pass. I'm leaving this place, and I'm not coming back.

* * *

*Ivan*

Ah, what the hell.

Back up is coming, and though Ivan would use the term loosely, he'll be glad when they arrive. For once, he doesn't want to be the guy that cleans up the mess. This time, he just wants to be the guy who goes home, pours himself a drink, and enjoys sipping it alone in silence.

There's a certain comfort in loneliness when it's all you've known for so long. Ivan'll never say he doesn't care about anybody, but damn it to hell if it's not nice to only be responsible for himself.

But looking over at Jill makes him feel different. He thinks she's going to need somebody eventually. Maybe she could be the person he finally begins to relate to. He promised to himself he'd never feel that much for anybody, and he meant it, but a person like him could use a friend sometimes.

The sirens roar up, the flashing lights bring Ivan out of his thoughts, and he looks around at everybody he knows.

"Body's in the basement," is all he says, and their excitement halts immediately.

They sulk their way into the cabin, either disappointed that they missed the action or hurt by the loss of somebody some of them may have called a friend.

Their days of firefights and car chases may never come, but if that dream is all that keeps them in the job, then so be it. They can live their lives in disappointment.

After the initial rush of officers comes the ambulance, and immediately paramedics have Jill inside on a stretcher and are looking at her toe with concern.

"Could be a nasty infection coming your way," Ivan hears one of them say, searching through a drawer for antibiotics.

He tries to give Jill a caring, assuring smile, but he just can't muster it. There's nothing to smile about. But she does the last thing Ivan could have ever expected from anybody, ever, in her position. She smiles at him, she nods, and she looks back down at her wounds without letting the smile fade.

It could be that she's lost too much blood, or that she's just happy to have gotten out of that basement, but Ivan thinks it's clear. Out of the three of them, who've all suffered in some way before, she's just the only one who learned how to do it without losing the most important facet of her personality: her resolve to smile through the rough times, to keep the bitterness at bay.

* * *

I've always admired those who could admit their own mistakes. I've tried and tried to fess up to the one big thing I did wrong, the one thing that turned me into whatever I am now, but I never really saw it. After my wife died, I let myself break. I completely gave up on being anything and caring about anything. Allowing the devil into your home is easy; it's getting him to leave that is the hard part. I was never good at kicking people out.

I managed to get back to the highway before meeting any police cars on the road up to Larry's cabin. Back in Prair Pass, I head north off the highway, in to the less desirable bit of town. Last time I was around here, it was to retrieve my wallet and liberate a dog named Max. It seems like a long time ago, though I know it wasn't. There's apartment buildings, alleyways, and parking structures. Plenty of places to hide. Plenty of places to run.

I pull up to the curb in front of an alley and sit for a while.

At some point, I became something my late wife wouldn't have been proud of. I've developed a warped view of right and wrong, apparently. Half of the time, I don't even know who the hell I am anymore.

All I know is she wouldn't like me very much. Not now.

It's difficult having lost someone you loved with everything you had, and then this whole new person comes into your life and creates similar feelings. It feels like a betrayal, in a way. Not because the love lost would be unhappy with you for moving on and finding happiness in life, but because you didn't think you would, didn't *want* to, feel those things ever again. It's too hard.

Losing it the first time killed the best parts of me. I'm a selfish bastard, but I'm glad I don't have to bear that again. We're inherently selfish creatures, humans—at least, I think so. It's not natural for us to care for others; it's just so deeply ingrained in our society that we should. We pretend and pretend and pretend, and when we've pretended enough, maybe we start to really care, or maybe we've just grown good enough at pretending that we even manage to fool ourselves.

I guess I've gotten pretty damn good at pretending.

I untie and re-tie my running shoes, good and tight, and step out of my car, stretching my back and tightening my running shorts.

The cops will be coming any minute now. There aren't a lot of places to look for a person in Prair Pass. Unfortunately for them, I won't be making it easy. I know what I deserve, what the price is for my actions, and I fully intend to pay it. But it's going to be at my own hand. Things are coming full circle, and there's something beautiful in that.

\* \* \*

*Ivan*

The questions keep on coming, but Ivan stays silent for the most part, whispering, "I don't know" every once in a while.

"Ivan, how did he get away? Were you here when the gunshot occurred? Was anyone else involved?"

"I don't know."

He supposes he may be playing up the shock a bit. Actually, he is absolutely playing up the shock. But he's committed to this role now, and he's not going to back out at this point.

They have his address. Most of the officers have already sped off to find him. Ivan knows he won't be there. He'll be long gone, but they don't have to know that.

He knows how this is all going to end, and in a strange way, he can take comfort in that. No more surprises from here on out. We can only hope.

The questions continue, but he's not listening anymore. In his head, he's far away, and all of this has been blown over for some time. He's warm and comfortable with a drink in his hand and sunglasses sliding down his nose from sweat on his face. Shit, he could almost be so bold as to say he's *happy* in this place.

"I think I'll stay for a while," he says out loud.

"I think that's a good idea, Ivan," Laura says, offering a sympathetic smile. "You seem pretty shaken up. Haven't really been you for a while, have you?"

"I . . . you know, I guess you're right," Ivan answers.

Laura lays a hand gently on his shoulder. He doesn't shy away from it. In fact, he finds some comfort there.

"I'm gonna stick around here with you, alright?" she asks.

Ivan nods, a smile peering through his tired features.

"Thanks, Laura."

A momentary concern at the fact that he may appear insane is extinguished quickly. He lets his head lull back, eyes closed, and smiles up at the beautifully rising sun.

Maybe it's his turn to just . . . not care.

\* \* \*

*Jill*

Perhaps this is my fault for trusting somebody so quickly, Jill thinks. But why should it have to be so difficult a thing, to put your faith in a person?

It's hard to care about someone but also never want to see them again, because seeing them would just hurt too much, bring back feelings that nobody should have to feel. Jill loved him. Maybe she still does. Maybe that's why this just sucks so much.

She is still sitting in the back of the ambulance, her foot elevated on the stretcher, some pills rattling around in a bottle pressed in to her right hand by the paramedic. She sees officers going in and out of the house where she very well could have taken her final breath. Ivan is leaning back against his car, a tall blonde cop rests her hand on his shoulder. Jill is grateful to be alive.

She doesn't know where he is, or where he's going, and she's trying not to permit herself to care. Letting go is something Jill learned young, and she'd like to think she's gotten pretty good at it. She was alone before, and she can be alone again, but she doesn't think he is going to be all right, not this time.

But Jill can't concern herself with that. His issues are his own, now, and her problems will be her own. She thinks she's fine with that. She would almost venture to say she's excited, if just a little bit. Things can be so much easier when you only have to be responsible for yourself.

She will miss him, and she'd be lying to herself if she thought she didn't want him to miss her too.

We all want to be loved, and cherished, and missed when we're gone. We've got this big idea that we're so important to the universe—for some people, it's all that keeps them going. Instead, she hopes for nothing, and takes comfort in the fact that in a hundred years nobody will remember or give a damn about what she's done. In the end, she can just slip out the door quietly and have her peace with a life that was good to her—for the most part, at least.

Hopefully, he can reach peace with himself. If there were one last thing Jill would wish for him, it would be that.

She sees Ivan staring up at the sky, searching for something, perhaps, and she looks for herself. She doesn't find anything there, besides the clouds and the blue, but that's all right.

\* \* \*

I've been running for a long time.

A deep wheeze accompanies every struggling breath, and my chest is riddled with painful cramps. My body, my brain, and every other bit of me in between are so very tired. I'm going to have to stop soon, but I know that they won't. The flashing blue and red shows up at the end of every alley, and I need to find another course.

I'm running out of options.

I'm surrounded by parking structures filled with excellent hiding places, and I decide it's time to get off the streets before I collapse.

The back doors to these places seem to be the type that are rarely locked, but as my luck would have it, the first one I try is impossible to pry open, whether due to my recent weakness or a lock on the other side, I am not sure. The second is locked as well, and my heart is pounding with fear by the time I crack open the third and hear heavily booted footsteps pursuing close behind me.

The structure is dark and smelly. I immediately begin searching for somewhere to hide, if only for a while, so I can regain my breath. But there's nowhere to hide. A beaten up old Chrysler is the only thing I see apart from the cold concrete walls and up ramps. I slide the deadbolt into the door and carry on upwards, taking the only route I've got left. Every floor is just as barren as the last. When I reach the third, I hear the door cave in two floors below me, the police continuing their pursuit with a newfound energy.

I still haven't devised a plan. There is only one floor left between me and the open sky. I could double back on the stairs, try to get back to the ground floor and make a break for it, but I won't. My final lap is coming to a close. I'm sure they're guarding every door to the stairs. The door ten feet in front of me bursts open to confirm my suspicions. Pistols are pointed directly at me. I'm being shouted at, told to freeze, but of course I can't do that now. I duck behind a pillar of concrete.

The squad of police following me through the floors is close behind, and I know my time is running out.

I consider surrendering, accepting the justice that I've been so adamant about trying to enforce. I almost smile at the thought, but I'm not going to do that. My job is nearly done. Murder is murder, and my principles have already dictated what happens to murderers. My punishment will be my own. The top floor is so close above me. If only I could have made it there. But this will have to do.

The gaps in the concrete form an empty space something like a window, and I can see the outside world clearly through it. I know what I have to do.

"Non-lethal force, people!" I hear shouted behind me as I begin my final sprint towards the window. It's too small for me to stand straight up in, but when I reach it, I climb up into a crouching position on the edge, looking down at the street below me. Four stories, probably about fifty-five feet.

Part of me has always known that this is the way it would have to end. I did what I thought was right. I feel I've made the world a better place, at least for a few people. It came with a cost, though, as things of importance always do. This time, a smile really does break out across my face. I look back at the police now gathered behind me, with their guns at their sides, and I apologize sincerely. I've made their jobs difficult tonight.

I look down at the concrete I'm about to get incredibly personal with, prepared for my own retribution, the only evildoer left on my list. I've realized that the longest suffering is that of a long and healthy life, and I'm glad to be ending mine now. I let go of everything. I relax all my muscles for the first time in what feels like an eternity, and I simply let myself fall.

My wife, who I never ventured to hope I could see again, meets me with an open palm and loving smile. I'm certain I'm just hallucinating, my mind finally breaking in the brief seconds before it explodes against the cement.

It gives me more comfort than I could ever ask for. More than I deserve.

* * *

*Ivan*

They found the bodies littered through the land surrounding Larry's cabin, and of course, they had to call Ivan in to help wrap up the case. Two young ladies from the city who went missing on a night out several months ago; the vet from twelve miles down the road, she'd been gone for years now; and the old British woman named

Nola who up and disappeared from her farm one evening without anyone but her neighbor and Laura Dintly taking much notice.

When Nola Kemping's body was confirmed to be one of the deceased, Laura Dintly's whole body visibly relaxed. Her immaculate posture released itself, a sigh of relief leaving her. Then, when the relief passed, she began to cry. Not big, body wracking sobs, but a few strong silent tears. She didn't move to wipe them away, she simply walked away from the body to her car, picked up her notebook, and ripped out a page. She balled the paper up, threw it on her passenger seat, and leaned against the hood of her cruiser. There was a finality to what she did. It appeared to be something that she'd been waiting on for a long time.

None of them deserved it, but that didn't stop Larry from ending their lives in brutal and horrific ways.

Does that make him deserving of the end he met? Who's to say, really? Not Ivan, that's for damn sure. But he met it, regardless of if it was deserved. That's the way it goes, more often than not, as far as Ivan could guess.

But his crazy new friend was right; Larry had killed those women, and he'd likely planned to do the same to Jill, but his new friend managed to stop Larry's heinous crimes for good. Ivan had worked alongside a murdering lunatic for years without a clue in his mind, save for some small bouts of hatred.

Too much for Ivan to even try thinking about right now.

The four bodies were found in a diamond shape around the cabin, about one hundred meters out, which tells him that Larry may have had some sort of method to his madness. The cops wouldn't have found them at all if Ivan hadn't recommended they search Larry's house for the map. The placement was exact. Someone would be assigned to read all the notebooks also found at the house, but it wouldn't be him. He'd had enough of all this.

It's a strange feeling when somebody you knew—even if you hated the person deeply—is now dead and gone from the world. He doesn't miss Larry, and he never will, but it still brings to light some respect for the fragility of life. Especially, he would suppose, in this case, where they have also found four other bodies.

Perhaps he was doing the right thing when he put a bullet through Larry's brain and blew bits of his skull all over the wall. Perhaps he was a lesser evil, put in place specifically to rid the world of something worse.

Nobody's innocent in this scenario. Hell, nobody's innocent in this life. We're all some form of filth spread throughout the galaxy, arrogant enough to think we're important, to think that we have this life thing, this good and evil thing, figured out.

Ivan can't help but think, as he takes in his surroundings, that we're just missing the point.

CPSIA information can be obtained
at www.ICGtesting.com
Printed in the USA
LVHW04s2311040518
576074LV00001B/5/P

9 781525 503429